STACEY in the HANDS of an ANGRY GOD

Thomas Keech

BOOK 1
of the Red State/Blue State
Confessions

ISBN 9780998380537 Hardback
ISBN 9781733052443 Paperback
ISBN 9781733052450 Ebook

Library of Congress Control Number
2019910538

Published by

Real
Nice Books
11 Dutton Court
Baltimore, Maryland 21228
www.realnicebooks.com

*Publisher's note: This is a work of fiction. Names, characters,
places, institutions, and incidents are entirely the product
of the author's imagination or are used fictitiously, and any
resemblance to actual persons, living or dead, or to events,
incidents, institutions, or places is entirely coincidental.*

Cover photo by Waldir Santos.
Cover art and design by Vanessa Snyder.
Set in Sabon.

For Joe

ALSO BY THOMAS KEECH:

The Crawlspace Conspiracy
Prey for Love
Hot Box in the Pizza District
Doc Doc Zeus: A Novel of White Coat Crime

Chapter 1

The right of a citizen to travel from one state to another is not found in the text of the United States Constitution. This court will not interfere with the Kansas legislature's authority to restrict the travel of its pregnant female citizens. – Meuller v. Adams, 620 U.S. 1966, 1984 (2024).

The wall of windows to the west was smudged with the nervous handprints of the women who waited there. The merciless glare of the sun painted the passengers orange. Stacey Davenport had forgotten to bring her note – and now found herself in the crush of female passengers in the crowded Conception Clearance lounge of Topeka-Jehovah International Airport. All the seats were taken. Conception Clearance was taking its time. A couple close to her was bickering.

"It's the *one* thing I asked you to do, and you forget it?" the middle-aged woman scolded her husband.

Almost everyone in Conception Clearance could hear her complaint. Half the women seated there smirked in sympathy with the unhappy wife. Of course, no one would be in Clearance unless they had forgotten something, usually the doctor's note required of any female of childbearing age who wished to travel from Kansas to a blue state. Verification of non-pregnancy was required. Notification of this requirement was posted online. Airport personnel had little patience for those who hadn't read it.

"Now she has to go into that … *room*," the woman muttered. "She's twelve, for God's sake. She's not ready for that kind of examination."

"Oh, honey, stop exaggerating." Her husband's voice was even lower. "It's no big deal. They just rub that goop on your tummy and slide that thing around. They can do it in a couple of minutes."

"She'll be in their control. That's what I'm afraid of."

The couple's griping continued as Stacey checked the time. Stacey was a third-year law student, and she knew the penalty for violation of the new travel laws, but she didn't think the twelve-year-old girl would be in any danger. And Stacey wasn't stupid; she and Grant had always been very careful. She had just forgotten to bring the note. This was a problem she could easily overcome if she could get through Conception Clearance in time to catch the plane. But she had to catch that plane. Grant was waiting in Boston, and she could tell his patience was wearing thin.

A sudden sob from the Clearance tent drew everyone's attention. A man in the brown uniform of Conception Control pulled a distraught woman from the exit side of the tent, handcuffed her wrists behind her and, with one hand on her shoulder from behind, rushed her toward the Security Office. She turned her head and frantically scanned the crowd. One man seemed to meet her eyes for a second before quickly looking down. The uniformed officer pulled a dark purple hood out of a leather pocket attached to his belt, stretched it over her head and steered her even more quickly away. The crowd stayed frozen in their seats. The penalty for a first offense was incarceration until the baby was born. Aiding and abetting was a felony.

Stacey could hardly blame Grant for wanting to stay in Boston. They'd met in college there. A native New Englander, he'd helped show the new girl from Kansas the blue state ropes. They were friends for years before they became lovers. But now they'd lived apart for two long years while she went to law school in her home state of Kansas. Grant was a year older than her and was already a lawyer for a tech startup in Boston that was doing well. They communicated daily by phone, text, e-mails and Instagram, and on whatever new app his tech clients back in Massachusetts were currently letting him try out.

Stacey had been rejected by eight law schools in New England. Her attitude, as Grant constantly explained to her, was the problem. Her problem, as she constantly explained to Grant, was her refusal to censor her every thought so as to conform to the latest in blue state political correctness. She finally applied for and was accepted by Kansas University Law School. She hadn't planned on ever going back home to Kansas, but she was accepted at KU and was determined to have a career in law. But it was coming to the point where she'd have to work things out with Grant. Fortunately, she had no doubt that Grant loved her. Grant loved her, even though he knew her well and understood what he was getting into with her. He was the only one on the east coast who knew the sordid story of her family's self-destruction, the only one she had shown the tracks on her arms.

"Examination Station Four is now available."

Stacey jumped up to beat the twelve-year-old girl to the spot. Her plane was leaving in twenty minutes. She reached Station Four and slipped through the white, tent-like flaps before the griping mother and inept father could get themselves together and present their daughter to the matron.

Stacey held her phone over the scanner at the entrance to the tent. Just as her identity registered on the matron's screen and Stacey was about to put it away, her phone dinged with an actual phone call. She didn't look to see who was calling. The matron, a thickset, thirty-something blonde with a green smock and a ponytail, eyed her with the resigned air of a government employee who had been called back early from her break.

Stacey had always brought a doctor's note and had never been required to submit to a Conception Control examination at the airport before. They were checking only for pregnancy, but she still hoped she wouldn't have to have to roll up her sleeves. She cringed at the thought of being judged yet again for the mistakes of her youth. She knew it was wrong, this craving to start with a clean slate, even if only in momentary interactions with strangers. She'd learned in countless rehabilitation meetings that she shouldn't hide even for a moment that she was an addict and would always be one. To hide this fact was to deny your true self, she'd learned. Still, she wasn't going to roll up her sleeves or take her blouse off unless she had to.

But the matron just nodded toward the examination table. Stacey did not have the time to risk antagonizing her. She handed her phone over to her without even looking to see who was calling. To make things go even quicker, she also handed the matron her pocketbook, removed her belt, opened her skirt, slid it down, lay down on the rustling hygienic paper of the examination table, and pushed her panties down as far as she hoped they'd have to go. The matron smiled weakly when she saw that Stacey had read the pamphlet and already knew the drill. She skipped all the preliminaries and squeezed the cool gel onto Stacey's skin, then ran the probe in slow concentric circles on her abdomen. That's all they needed to do, the pamphlet said, and the process was usually over within about five minutes.

"Damn. What the ...?" The matron picked up the head of the probe and stared at it like it was clogged with something she might be able to poke out with her finger. *Hurry. Please hurry.* Stacey mouthed the words but didn't dare say them. She didn't ask for an explanation. Any explanation would take too long. The woman shrugged and walked out of the room.

Stacey's phone dinged again. She looked. Her mother. Couldn't her mother hold things together for just one weekend? She decided not to answer it. She heard the preliminary boarding call for her plane, and she decided to remain frozen in the examining position on the table so as to not lose one more second when the matron came back. The matron did come back in a minute and slid the probe over Stacey's skin again. Then she picked up the probe once more, looked at it closely, and actually did poke the head of it with her finger. She looked Stacey in the eyes, shrugged.

"Is it working now?" Stacey ventured.

"Yeah. It's fine. I guess." She took Stacey's phone, held it up to a different scanner on her desk, tapped a few keys. But before she tapped the final "enter" key, she stopped, held her finger over the keyboard, turned and stared at Stacey. "All praise to the Lord God Almighty."

Everyone in Kansas knew the call and response. Though not legally required, it was often the only way to get a state employee to act promptly. "And blessed be His holy Prophet, Reverend James Ezekial." She mumbled the words. Her tone of voice cost her an extra few seconds before the matron turned back and finally tapped the enter key. "You're cleared to leave the great state of Kansas."

Stacey wiped the gunk off her stomach, slid off the table, pulled her clothes on, grabbed her pocketbook, and began to run towards her gate. She rushed down the sloping concrete entrance to Pier B. The new airport had been built in 2023 and was just one year old, but the air conditioning in the terminal wasn't keeping up with the blazing August heat. Her blouse was sticky with sweat.

She reached the gate ten minutes after the boarding call, but she still had to wait for 360 people to pass the last security clearance, then for 720 carry-on bags to be stuffed into the overhead compartments. Stacey couldn't afford to check her bags, considering she had to change planes in Chicago and the total baggage fees for the trip would be $300 each way. She once told Grant it might be cheaper just to buy new clothes at each destination. Grant had said as far as he was concerned, she didn't have to wear any clothes at all. She had given him a polite laugh, enjoying her status as the only woman in Massachusetts he could legally kid like that.

For now, she'd just have to fight it out with the other passengers. She was glad she was tall, five feet seven, and could reach the bins herself. She had just successfully jammed her backpack into a tiny crevice between two hard suitcases in the overhead bin when her phone rang again. She put it on speaker, then immediately regretted it as she heard her mother's squawk.

"Stacey!" Stacey was used to dealing with her mother. She was used to guiding her mother through crises, step by step. But Stacey was now blocking a whole line of passengers. She couldn't stop to babysit her mother. She reached her assigned row and tried to slide around the protruding knees of the portly man in the aisle seat just as he tried to stand up to let her through. They mistimed the maneuver and squished together, belly to belly. She lost her balance and fell – as far as there was room to fall – into the narrow slot between the seat cushions and the backs of the seats in the previous row. Her phone landed on the floor.

"Oh, excuse me."

"What!" Stacey heard her mother's screech coming out of the phone.

"Not you, Mom." Stacey's head was now halfway in the lap of the woman in the window seat. The woman instinctively reached out to hold her from slipping all the way down to the floor. Amazingly, she smiled at the awkward situation. The man managed to stand up and untangle his legs from hers and move into the aisle so she could wriggle herself onto a seat and push herself up. Then they all sat down. Everybody quietly composed themselves without looking each other in the eye.

"Stacey!"

"Oh. Um … Ma'am, can I ask you to reach my phone for me?" None of them could actually see the floor. The woman felt around on the floor with her hand, then handed her the phone, still without making eye contact. Stacey quickly switched off the speaker phone.

"The police just came and took your brother Kendrick's computer!"

"What? Mom, calm down. The police? You mean Randy? Randy took Kendrick's computer? Why?"

"*Uncle* Randy to you. No. Not him. The *Kansas* police, the KBI."

Stacey racked her brain for what she had learned about search and seizure in her first year of law school. She had aced criminal law without giving even a passing thought to practicing that dirty, unprofitable business.

"Kendrick's still there? They didn't arrest him?"

"No."

"Oh. Good."

That's all you can come up with? Stacey could hear her mother's unspoken criticism. But her mother didn't have the nerve to actually say it. So Stacey plowed on. "Is he okay?"

"He's in his room. He won't come out. He won't talk to anybody."

It was hard to believe her mother had ever qualified to be a custodial parent. Stacey had watched her mother go downhill, practically turn her brain off in the face of her husband's desertion. When Stacey's father had decided he loved OxyContin more than his family, her mother had tried to hold them together with her administrative assistant's salary, her bursts of inconsistent economizing, and a lot of useless whining and haranguing. Then, after so many harsh laws were forced on everyone in Kansas by Reverend Ezekial and the Certainty Party, Audrey seemed to go into spells of erratic, impotent frenzy. Nothing ever seemed to be going right for her mother. Her father, between stints in rehab, sometimes forced his way into the house at night and slept in the summer kitchen. Meanwhile, her little sister Amy had lately turned moody and snotty.

"Okay, okay, Mom. You said the police took Kendrick's

computer. Why? What did they say?"

"They didn't say anything."

"Did you read the warrant?"

"They didn't say anything about a warrant."

"Mom, the police can't search your house without a warrant."

"Nobody said anything about a warrant."

Of course, there were certain situations where you didn't need a warrant any more, but Stacey knew better than to tell her mother about that. These were mostly situations where people were in imminent danger – or in cases of terrorism. But Stacey knew the Supreme Court had recently ruled that each state could define for itself what constituted terrorism. There seemed to be no limit to the states' authority to define new crimes.

Her mother's past harangues about the Certainty Party's evil enactments had fallen on deaf ears. Had the Certainty Party redefined terrorism in Kansas? Could the new Feto-Terrorism law possibly apply to Kendrick? The new laws pushed by Reverend Ezekial and the Certainty Party had been so numerous, and had come on so fast, that Stacey hadn't been able to keep track of them all. She'd been so busy, determined to keep clean, edit law review, graduate with honors, make it to the partner track of a big firm somewhere and keep her relationship with Grant alive, that she didn't know nearly as much about the oppressive new CP laws as she should have.

Her mother interrupted this train of thought. "Randy says it won't come to anything." Randy, her mother's cousin, was the sheriff in Cosgrove, the tiny town her family lived in thirty miles south of Stacey's current apartment in Lawrence. "Randy said when they take computers, it's usually for child porn. You know, I worry like crazy about what Kendrick is up to in his room all the time. But Randy says they can't get your brother for child porn because he's … he's legally still a child himself.

Funny, huh?"

It wasn't a child porn investigation, Stacey was sure. But she wouldn't tell her mother that, at least not right now. "What are you doing about it?"

"Oh, honey, I don't know."

"You have to do something, Mom. Where's Amy?"

Her mother's voice dropped. "Oh honey, I don't know. Something's happened to Amy, too. Your sister hasn't talked to anybody for two days. She won't let anybody in her room, and she won't come out. I listen at the door. I can hear her crying. Can't you come home?"

Her mother's solution for every problem was come back, Stacey, come back and take over this wreck of a family, help me, don't make *me* act like the grownup. No more. "I have to leave, Mom. It's just for a few days. I have to leave."

"We need legal help … somehow. I've got no money for a lawyer."

"Mom, I'm already on the plane. And I'm not a lawyer. I'm just a law student. I can't represent anyone."

"Oh, honey, I don't know."

"You *do* know, Mom. You know he needs a lawyer, right now. Okay. Listen, when I get to Boston I'll ask Grant if he can help. With the money. Okay? So just go do it, Mom. This isn't a joke."

"Oh. Alright, honey."

"Now go call a lawyer and get him to talk to Kendrick right away. Tell Amy I want to talk to her. I'll try to help out when I get back."

Her mother's voice went sour. "You're always happy to be getting away from us."

"Goodbye, Mom."

** ***

Grant, in his first law job, was putting in fourteen-hour days for Liotech back in Boston, but he still managed to come out to Lawrence almost once a month to see Stacey. Generally, they hid out and played in the bedroom of her garden apartment not two blocks from Kansas University Law School where Stacey had just finished her second year, coming out only for walks around the campus and around Lawrence and occasional trips to her hometown of Cosgrove, thirty miles away.

They would soon be going into their third year of separation. He was into tech law, and there had been no great prospects for success in that field in Kansas when he graduated. Passing up on a few more lucrative offers, he had taken the job as the sole counsel for tiny Liotech in Boston because he liked the owners and he wanted to get in on the ground floor of their startup.

She remembered their last phone conversation almost word for word.

"It's getting to me, Stacey, you being so far away. I miss you. Can you please come out here this weekend?" When she didn't answer, he added, "We have to make a decision."

"Oh." She understood from his tone what he meant. He was not willing to wait forever. He was too sane to wait forever. Too balanced. Not like anyone she had grown up with. The self-assurance she had fought for every moment of her life had been given to him free at birth.

She told herself she didn't feel guilty about causing their separation. Yes, she had gone back to Kansas after college, but only because she gave up on being admitted to an eastern law school. Several times in college she had been guilty of what they called "micro-aggressions," and she had even been taken to Student Disciplinary Court once for refusing to remove the word "oriental" from a history paper. It seemed to her that words that were perfectly acceptable one day were considered offensive the next. A lot of her fellow college students in Massachusetts seemed be in a state of constantly feeling offended. There were even courses that taught them how to find offense almost everywhere. The whole atmosphere annoyed her.

After she had graduated from college, she could have gotten a non-legal job in Boston that would have allowed her to live with Grant. But Stacey had learned from her mother's bad example that you have to go for what you want in life, with or without a man. She refused to take any old white-collar job in any state just to be with Grant. Stacey had seen her mother let herself be dragged down into the muck by hitching herself to the wrong man.

If Grant had whined like her mother or screamed like her sister or mumbled and hung up the phone like her father, Stacey would not have gotten so upset when he complained about their separation. She had gradually realized that Grant's way of communicating was the normal way. He said what he meant, usually only once, and so you had to listen. It had been a new experience for her, talking with him, because he was actually there in front of you and not far away in some psychic uproar of his own that blocked out whatever you were saying. She wasn't used to being really listened to, and she loved it. But it was scary too, because he always meant what he said. He was a good man, and a sane man, and she was not afraid of that any more, and she had convinced herself that she deserved him.

They had been confidants for a long time before they started dating. She had seen he was hesitating to step over the line, weighing chancing a romance against losing a friend. She had been hesitating, too. She could be a friend to him at a certain distance without revealing everything. Being lovers would be different. One April afternoon, as they were lounging in her dorm room having one of their long daily conversations, conversations that were piquant and stimulating but lately tinged with tension, she suddenly stood up. Slowly, as they talked, meeting his eyes, she began to unbutton her blouse, first at the cuffs and then down the front. She was trembling. He smiled and stepped forward to embrace her.

"No. Wait."

She stepped back, finished unbuttoning and pulled the blouse loose from the waist. Then she took it off completely and stood looking at him, not trembling any more but challenging him with her eyes. She held herself so he could plainly see the needle tracks on her arms.

"Oh. My. God. Stacey, I had no idea."

"I had a really bad time in high school, after my Dad left. Valium, OxyContin, then heroin, then anything. I was on methadone the whole first year I was here in college. I still go to meetings sometimes."

"Why didn't you tell me until now?"

"I don't know. I sort of want to keep it a secret. I keep thinking about what's happening back in Kansas. They're really rough on addicts there now."

He never asked her for any details, but he insisted on driving her to her NA meetings. She knew this wasn't the way lovers related to each other in movies, or in books. But they did become lovers, though she always suspected she was more smitten than he was. She knew she was some sort of add-on to his life, a plug-in to his operating system. If she was removed, he would be heartbroken. He wouldn't be able to function for a while. But he had grown up in a normal family and had a ton of friends, and he now had a legal assistant named Lacee who seemed to be in love with him – though he was so used to being loved he had hardly noticed yet. She knew in her heart that if they ever split up, he would get over his sorrow some day and find someone else. She would survive, too. She would be a successful unmarried lawyer and run a sane household and dole out enough money to keep her family from slipping totally off the edge – hopefully from far enough away so they wouldn't be able to pull her back into the muck.

*** ***

Stacey powered off her cell phone and tablet while drinking a diet soda in a bar in O'Hare Airport in Chicago, waiting for her connecting flight. She had learned over the past several years that turning her back on problems was a bad habit, but she felt she needed just a few minutes' respite. She tried to close her eyes, but they popped open when she heard that voice on the giant TV screen facing her across the bar. Reverend James Ezekial himself was being interviewed on a nationwide talk show.

"We are talking with Reverend James Ezekial, a minister from Neola County, Kansas, who recently made headlines for his proposed massive Bible Land Housing Project, scheduled to be the largest development ever in that state. But today, I want to talk about your political movement, the Certainty Party. The Certainty Party has quickly gained a majority in both houses of the Kansas legislature. To what do you attribute your sudden political success?"

Ezekial sat alone at table across from the interviewer. For someone who claimed to be in direct contact with God, he didn't look anything like the gaunt, ascetic prophet his name conjured. He seemed to be of average size, a little husky, with a round face, thick-framed, horn-rimmed glasses and an untamed brown comb over. His dark blue suit had a large scarlet cross emblazoned across the breast pocket. He seemed to be looking at a point above and beyond the camera, as if he were constantly receiving messages from on high.

"Rachel, the Certainty Party is not a political movement. It is a manifestation of God's grace. Under his direct guidance, we are remaking the state of Kansas in His image."

Rachel York, the attractive young interviewer, met his eyes, pursed her lips and nodded noncommittally.

"Not a political movement? But hasn't the Certainty Party

passed a record number of bills on women's rights and family law?"

"God has done so."

"But it's your Certainty Party that has passed these laws."

"I am an instrument of God. He has shown me the Way. Those who follow me will have inner peace forever."

"Okay. Well, let's talk about what the Certainty Party has done. They have successfully enacted two radical laws, the Feto-Terrorism and Conception Control laws. What do you say to those who claim you are taking back all the rights women have gained in the last hundred years?"

"Here's what I say. The Bible goes back *four thousand* years. Everything we need to know is in that book! You follow the book, you're following the law of God!"

Ezekial turned to the interviewer, smiled warmly, and softened his tone. "Rachel, you seem like a good person. But I'm sure you feel a little anxious sometimes. I'm sure there are times when you can't see clearly the path ahead. But the answers are simpler than you think. If you welcome God into your life, He will bring you the inner peace you crave. He will bring you, above all, the Certainty that you are following God's path, the only path that will bring you happiness. I can show you that path."

"I definitely will consider that. Thank you, Reverend Ezekial." Rachel turned her engaging smile to the camera. "And when we come back after the break, we'll bring you a story that may challenge one of the fundamental beliefs many of us base our daily lives upon. We'll talk with a nutritionist who will explain his research that shows, he claims, that kale is *not* good for you!"

*** ***

She got more of the story of the seizure of Kendrick's computer as she waited at the gate at O'Hare. Her mother's second call had little actual content, except that Randy had helped her get a lawyer for Kendrick. Randy, her mother's cousin, was the sheriff of Cosgrove, but he wasn't permitted to intervene officially on Kendrick's behalf because he was a relative. Stacey's father could not be found. Stacey calmed her mother down enough to get her off the phone. Stacey sometimes wished she were ten years older and had money, and connections, and a way to help her mother – from a distance.

The police taking Kendrick's computer without a warrant was really a bad sign. She frantically researched the website of the Kansas House of Representatives on her phone. She hadn't realized until she saw the TV interview a few minutes before that Reverend Ezekial's Certainty Party, which had won the majority of seats in the legislature in the last election, had actually enacted so many of the controversial "Laws of God" he preached about almost every day on his podcast, *The Prophet*. The CP's first major accomplishment had been called "An Act Against Feto-Terrorism." This act redefined a term in the English language. The term "terrorism" now included a whole list of behaviors related to women's reproduction. All of them were now felonies. One of those new terrorist crimes was providing information to a pregnant female that might facilitate her obtaining an abortion.

She clicked off the website and called her sister. It wasn't unusual for Amy to be avoiding her mother, but Stacey was sure she would answer her big sister's call.

"He's a terrorist?" Amy blurted out.

"Of course not."

"The lawyer said they could put him in jail for 20 years."

Stacey felt suddenly sick. Kendrick was fourteen and could have done anything on the internet. But terrorism? She was absolutely sure her lost-in-space little brother hadn't done anything deliberate that would get him in serious trouble. And he didn't even have a girlfriend.

She tried to focus on Amy. Stacey was the only person outside Amy's circle of pot-head friends whom her little sister would talk to now. Amy was fifteen.

"What about you, Amy? Mom said something happened to you?"

"Oh …. Nothing. Don't waste your time coming back here." Her voice went lifeless. "There's nobody here worth it."

"What happened to you?"

There was a long silence. "No, I can't talk," Amy finally managed. "I'm sorry." Then the phone clicked off. Stacey was hurt. Amy had never hung up on her before.

Unlike Amy, Stacey had at least a distant memory of happier times. The family had seemed normal, and Stacey, by far the oldest, had been her father's favorite. But now he was so far gone from her she literally couldn't pay him enough to treat her like a daughter. And she'd been as bad as he was. Stacey had never confessed her whole sordid drug history to anyone, not even Grant. But she would never forget that crushing depression, and that grinding need to escape – and what she did to escape. That all had been covered up, hidden in confidential juvenile records, forgotten in the drugged-out haze her then-friends now still lived in. Silenced within the family. But not within her mind. She knew she had no right to lecture anyone.

She turned off her phone an hour outside of Boston. A better daughter would have kept her line open. She still felt queasy. She'd been through this family turmoil before. The only person who thought she was doing right by her family was Grant. In Grant's simple view of life, if a family member needed help, you gave them that help, and they were grateful, and it worked. He had no idea about the psychic backdrops of her family life: questioned motives, lifelong resentments, bottomless despair.

He was waiting for her outside the security gates at Logan

Airport. She immediately spotted his head of dark, curly hair visible just above most in the crowd. His hazel eyes shone green in the evening sunlight slanting through the tall windows. He gave her a wide smile. She dropped her backpack and ran into his arms.

"I missed you," he murmured fervently into her ear, his touch on her back sending warmth through her body.

She drew her face back and kissed him hard and long. "I missed you so much." Years ago, he had helped her conquer her hesitation about kissing in public. He could still evoke in her a bit of that wonderful illusion that they were the center of the universe and the rest of the world could wait. And she hoped now they were at the center of something significant, something worth working at. She felt energized. She hurried toward the exit while Grant kept pace and carried her backpack.

"Oh, wait." She darted away toward the brightly lit blue kiosk. Every arrival gate in every blue state airport had at least one contraceptive kiosk for travelers from those states where contraception was illegal.

Grant wondered exactly what type of birth control she was going to use. Just the idea that she was getting ready for him sent him into an erotic reverie. But the weight of her backpack gradually pulled him out of his dream state. He noticed that she was taking a lot longer than the other customers, who all seemed to know exactly what they wanted. Well, it was none of his business. For three years now, he had worked joyously at discovering what she liked in bed.

"Sorry I took so long. Where's your car?"

It would be a ZipCar, she knew. Mister High-Tech lawyer would never use his own car in Boston, even if he could afford to keep one there. Besides, the ZipCar had a special place in their history, and he still showed a trace of a smile whenever the subject came up.

"What should we do?" he asked, smiling. "Are you hungry?

Dinner? First?"

"Yeah. I guess we could do that first."

He didn't pick up on her hesitation. Grant always moved surely in the direction he thought was right. That was one reason it was so easy to be around him. And did it matter, really, what they did first? They went to a sit-down pizza restaurant not far from his apartment in Beacon Hill. It had clean brick interior walls, and the dinner cost as much as a filet mignon feast would cost in Lawrence.

"Do you want dessert?"

"I want to go to your place. No. Wait. I need to tell you something first."

Grant sat back, eyes focused on her. "You're not breaking up with me?"

She was a little flustered by the mature steadiness in that gaze. He was a man who dealt with everything up front and who would not put off dealing with anything important. He would never hide, evade, try to forget. She wanted to be like that someday.

"No. It's this. I know you might be sick of my family and their troubles, but one more thing's happened. My little brother's computer has been seized by the state cops. Without a warrant. That means they're investigating terrorism."

"Oh crap! More problems at home." Then he caught himself. "I mean, what can we do?"

"Honestly, nothing. He has a criminal lawyer now. You know, he's fourteen. It's got to be some stupid shit he did on the internet. But I don't think it would be wise for me to talk to him about it."

"I agree. You could be subpoenaed and asked what he told you. It's creepy what states can do to you nowadays if they call it a terrorism case." Grant leaned in, spoke quietly. "I bet your mom's a mess."

Stacey smiled ruefully. "Yeah, she is. As usual." She took

a sip of her soda. "I don't think there's anything legal I can do for Kendrick right now." She took another sip and picked up the dessert menu and pretended to look at it.

Then she threw it down. Grant's self-confidence was catching, and she was suddenly unashamed of what she wanted. "Right now, what I really want to do is go to your apartment and get naked in your bed."

He hadn't forgotten what she liked. His touch felt new – again. And it was obvious how much he needed her.

"I love you, Grant."

After he was asleep, she made her way groggily to the bathroom.

Chapter 2

They got little sleep as they tried to make up for all their time apart. She knew Grant had had plenty of previous girl-friends. A lot of women admired his looks and physique. Tall, but not too tall. A nice mane of dark brown hair and those warm hazel eyes. But he seemed to feel he was average, just like everybody else, the same as anybody, normal – and so naturally he believed he was perfectly qualified to ask out any girl in the world, all of whom he thought were just as average and normal and appealing as he was. He told Stacey he couldn't understand why anyone would be nervous about dating. He had the same easygoing attitude about any situation, playing sports, goofing around in the dorms, joshing with other new people on a new job. He seemed comfortable in almost any role.

During Stacey's first year in college, when they were just friends, she used to tease him about his dating pattern. She saw him chat up girl after girl, dive into exclusive, very sexual relationships, then slowly back out. A lot of his girlfriends knew the game from the beginning. On those few occasions when there were tears, angry letters, mocking memes, he always seemed surprised. Well, she'd had fun, hadn't she? What was the problem?

"Tell me why," he once complained to Stacey after a new ex had posted a particularly nasty comment about him, "why can't people just have fun, enjoy each other and move on?"

Because they might not be people who *could* move on, she wanted to say. In her own family, there was no human interaction without serious drama. Her father, the most skilled machinist in his company, mysteriously lost his job when she was in high school. It took two years of explanations and denials – and outright lies – before she and her mother finally figured out that his real problem was drugs. Stacey still resented all that time she spent grasping for an innocent explanation.

The truth about her father had crushed her. She did nothing for two years but try to escape the pain. The only thing that worked was drugs. Prescription Valium, then prescription OxyContin, both easy to get, then heroin – first a wonderful feeling, then a blank feeling, then a craving for that blankness above all else. She couldn't remember half the things she did to get them, and she now lived in constant fear of finding out. It was pure luck that she wasn't now turning tricks in some crack house in Kansas City. Grant would never understand these lows or highs, or her constant, nagging remorse. To him, life was easy. As was romance. She'd never seen the beginnings and endings of romance handled with such *sangfroid* until she met Grant. Back when they were just friends, she had started calling him the ZipCar Dater, or just Zip for short.

*** ***

Looking for a late breakfast, they traipsed down the two flights of stairs out of his apartment and headed for another restaurant he knew, a place off the tourist track that looked a little worn around the edges.

"Oh. Right here? This place is near your work, isn't it? Do you eat here often on workdays?" Stacey asked.

"Not usually. At work, they want us to eat in. They supply free drinks, sometimes pizza too, if we do."

"Yeah. Because they want you to work fourteen hours a day, and they don't want to pay you overtime."

He smiled, shrugged. "That's the way the world is in big law," he joked. He didn't work for a big firm. He was company counsel, and the only attorney, for a tiny software firm. He told her he liked the owners, liked the start-up atmosphere, didn't mind learning on the job everything: corporate law, contracts, copyright, employee rights, figuring out how to get the company out of the lease they'd outgrown.

"It's tough," he went on, "But I think I learned more law here in the first six months than I ever did in three years of law school."

"It must be nice to be in the real world, getting paid real money. I can't wait to get my last year over with."

"The company is expanding like crazy. Mick and Amos really know what they're doing, as far as business goes."

She waited for him to stop bragging and talk about that touchy subject they had both been avoiding.

"Your internship –it's still going through?" he finally asked. She could tell he was trying to keep up a neutral face.

She had applied for an internship at Packer, Packer and Doe, the biggest firm in Topeka. She had the grades and law review, and the preliminary interview had gone well.

"I should know by next week. They were really encouraging, though. And they kept saying they always pick their new associates from their pool of past interns."

He took a breath. "Oh. That's great." But he didn't sound like that was great. His eyes shot over to the right. "Hold on. The waitress is coming."

"*Waitstaff*. Don't you even know how to speak Massachusetts, native son?"

The woman took their orders and briskly turned away as if she knew she was interrupting something.

His warm eyes focused on hers. "I don't want to lose you. But it's been almost two years we've been living like this. And if you get this internship and then later get hired at Packer, Packer and Doe in Topeka, what's to keep it from becoming permanent?"

"I know. I know. But I need this. Maybe it's hard for you to understand. You have a family that's great. And your parents, they're sane. They're not all in debt up to their ears. I have nothing."

"I can help. You know, financially."

Grant was already helping with her father. After her father had run through all the family's health insurance benefits, exhausted all their savings, taken out a second mortgage on their house to finance – he said – a third try at inpatient rehab, flunked out of rehab, stolen his wife's jewelry and everything moveable in the house, moved out of the house, double-crossed all his friends, even his addict friends, Stacey found him a cheap room on the second floor rear of an old wooden store in the next county. She ran out of money by the third month. Her mother refused to contribute a cent. Stacey didn't want to ask Grant for money, didn't want to be dependent on him, on anybody. But what choice did she have? She could almost feel her father's desperate need reaching back and touching her from the past, trading on their old love. She wanted that old love back so badly she couldn't resist. She had no choice. She took Grant's money. He had paid the rent on her father's room for over a year now.

"We could have so much fun if you would move here." His look was ardent.

"I want to. I mean …. Do you love me, Grant?"

"*Of course,* I love you. Remember we used to go out three nights a week, sleep in on Sundays? That was so great. Now, we'd have money, too. It would be even better."

It was nice that he said he loved her, even if his words got quickly buried in his reminiscences of their college days – days that were fun but that she did not want to repeat. Their college life seemed so trivial compared to what was happening now.

"What's happening to this country, Grant?"

"It's all right." He stroked her hand. "You and me, we'll be all right."

"I don't know. I think it's getting worse. Roland says …."

"Who's Roland?"

"Oh. I told you about him, didn't I? He's this guy, a little older. He's a law student, but he's also a state delegate." She decided not to mention he was drop-dead gorgeous. And that he lived in the apartment right above hers.

"Not a Certainty Party person, I hope."

"Of course not. He's an Independent. He hates the Certainty Party."

"The CP has a firm majority now, right?"

"Yeah, but Governor Adams is a Republican. She says she won't go along with the CP agenda."

"Your Governor Fanny Adams signed the Feto-Terrorism law. She signed Conception Control."

"But she says that's as far as she'll go. Getting any more of those anti-women laws passed will now have to be a three-step process: they'll pass a law, Governor Adams will veto it, and then they'll have to try to override her veto."

They dropped the political talk and walked the harbor. They bought food and wine to take back to his apartment for lunch. Two years ago, they'd decided to play it by ear, fly back and forth as much as they could afford to. Grant could afford it a lot more than she could, and he paid for the bulk of the flights. She hated that she was already financially dependent on him. She wouldn't have let him help with her father if she'd had any other choice. He'd done what no boyfriend should have to do, and he'd done it cheerfully. But she was losing control.

"I wish you would just come and get a legal job in Kansas," she griped.

"Mick and Amos really need me. I'm not bragging, but I think Liotech would go down the tubes in 60 days if I left. It's crazy busy. And they're starting to make real money."

"Why don't they hire more attorneys?"

"I'm asking them to, all the time. You know we did get this woman, Lacee, as my legal assistant, but she's not that much help yet. We don't even have the time to interview another lawyer."

His third-floor apartment in Beacon Hill was very expensive. They climbed the stairs carrying their purchases in his reusable canvas bags. Paper and plastic were both banned in Boston. He made one of his usual slapdash sandwiches on fresh-cut bread with cheese and meat and pickles and tomatoes. He handed her the wineglasses to fill and turned to get the sandwiches. He turned back.

"You only poured one glass?"

"I can't drink," she met his eyes. "I took a pregnancy test last night."

Chapter 3

State laws concerning "terrorism" deal with criminal offenses believed to be especially dangerous by the citizens of that state. These offenses might call for unusual precautions and may necessitate procedural shortcuts. We see no text in the Constitution that prohibits a state from classifying any particular crime into this category. – Schnitker v. Adams, 621 U. S. 440, 451 (2023).

Amy usually brought the food to Don herself, leaving it inside the unlocked door of his room on the second-floor back porch. It was an old, two-story, wooden building that used to have a general store on the first floor and quarters for renters on the second. The general store had long since closed and been replaced, in dying succession, by a pool hall, a laundromat, and a pizza parlor. Presently it was occupied by a store selling old vinyl records. There were two tiny apartments off the back second-floor porch. The porch and railing were painted a flaking grey. The old wood smelled dusty when it was dry and musty when it rained. The building was in Neola County, 25 miles west of their family home in Cosgrove. Stacey sent her sister $30 of her boyfriend's cash every week just to make the delivery to their father. Amy didn't have a license, but she would take her mother's truck anyway.

Amy hated these deliveries. Sometimes there were old guys hanging out in back, belching and spitting over the railing. Amy would never go up when they were there. She rarely saw her father there, but the food was usually gone by the next week. She absolutely refused to clean up the room, and so it gradually filled with pizza boxes, styrene food containers, and greasy papers until he got on one of his rehab kicks and cleaned it up. The whole situation was a mess, but Stacey had explained she couldn't give him a penny in cash because it would probably go right into his arm.

Amy had only reluctantly agreed to do these deliveries. When she was little, her father hadn't thought enough of her to tell her he was sick on drugs, hadn't thought enough of her to say goodbye to her when he left. She didn't know him now, and she didn't want to. Her status now was food-box delivery person. Each time she climbed the steps, she hoped he wouldn't be there so she could just slide the box inside the door.

"Why can't Mom do this?" she had complained to her older sister.

"We can't ask her to do it. He hurt her too much."

*** ***

Audrey told Amy that Harshaw, the lawyer she had hired after Kendrick's computer was seized by the police, wanted a family meeting about Kendrick's legal problem. Audrey made Amy choose the time and place – so her younger daughter would have no excuse not to come. This was her mother's way of manipulating her, she knew. Kendrick wouldn't be there.

Lawyer Harshaw was obviously not impressed with her mother's attempts to clean up the house. Amy smirked to see him hesitate before finally setting his large rump down on the sofa. Her mother dithered about whether he wanted a glass of water, a coaster, a pen, while Amy was so embarrassed she tried to blend in with the wallpaper.

"There's no easy way to say this. As soon as they draw up the papers, Kendrick will probably be charged with aiding and abetting Feto-Terrorism."

"Terrorism? He's fourteen! He wouldn't know a terrorist if he bumped into one on the street. He doesn't know about anything but video games and football."

Harshaw cleared his throat. "Unfortunately, the Supreme Court has left it up to the states to set out their own definition of terrorism. And in the last legislative session, dominated by the Certainty Party, they greatly expanded the definition. In Kansas, Feto-Terrorism is now defined to include obtaining information for a pregnant woman about abortion or related activities."

"We know that. But what are you talking about? Abortion? Kendrick's never even had a girlfriend."

"I didn't say he's charged with abortion. Actually, a male cannot be charged with abortion. I said he was charged with *providing information that may reasonably be interpreted as aiding a pregnant female to obtain an abortion or engage in abortion-related crimes*. That's still a felony. That's still terrorism."

"So, you mean, if he went on the internet or something ...?" Amy began, then stopped, her smooth brown bangs emphasizing her dark, intelligent eyes.

"That's right, young lady." Harshaw turned to her with an expression of relief on his round, bearded face. He finally had found someone who could understand these simple terms. "They've already analyzed his computer. They claim he was looking at websites that could be used to find centers for abortion procedures in blue states. That's aiding and abetting terrorism. I mean, it's aiding and abetting terrorism *if* there is a pregnant girl somewhere in the picture."

"That's totally stupid. He's afraid to even talk to girls," Amy pouted.

"That's good to hear, young lady. But you all need to listen to these instructions right now. Do not talk to each other about the case. I mean not about Kendrick, about his computer habits, about his girlfriends – not even about any friends of his, because he might have been doing it for one of his friends. Especially, do not talk to Kendrick. But do not talk to each other, either."

"Well, that part certainly won't be hard," her mother grumped.

Amy rolled her eyes. Audrey's sour sarcasm was tiring.

"Either of you might be called before the special grand jury. They can ask you anything, and you have to answer. But you need to talk to me first. *Do not talk to the police. They are not your friends.* Nothing you say to the police can get Kendrick out of trouble. But you can easily get him into more trouble. I am the only person you can safely talk to. So, once again, do not talk to anyone but me. Not to your neighbors or relatives, your friends, not to Kendrick, not to each other. This is the world we live in."

Chapter 4

She had never seen the color drain so quickly out of anyone's face. It was a minute before Grant muttered something, and she couldn't even understand what it was.

"What?" she said. It was the first time she had ever seen him lose his confidence. His hands were shaking. I should have known, she thought.

"I don't think you understand what this means," he said, louder this time.

"I think I know what being pregnant means," she snapped back. Then she tried to soften her tone. "Don't you love me? I was really hoping you'd be more excited."

"Of course, I love you. But here's what it means, Stacey." His voice was hard. "First of all, if you go back to Kansas, you can't come back here again, not until after the baby is born. That's Conception Control. And in Kansas your baby will be in danger of forced adoption."

"Oh, come on. That's only happening to poor mothers, drug addicts, people like that. There's not a chance in the world they'd do that to a law student."

"How about to a recovering drug addict?"

She looked at him. "That's low."

"I'm sorry. But Kansas has turned into a dangerous, creepy place, and I'm never living there."

He sat there swallowing his wine sip by sip, staring down at his hands when he wasn't drinking. She waited for him to talk, but he was in the middle of his second glass and there was no sign yet that he would even look at her. The future course of her life was being determined by this man who was now nervously sipping his wine. He didn't even like wine that much.

"You always say the most important thing in your life is

that we be together." She realized she was talking too fast, like desperate people do.

"That *the two of us* could be together." He pushed his chair back from the table.

"What are you saying?" She hadn't intended the harshness in her voice. She kept talking, trying to control the panic that she could now feel rising in her chest.

He suddenly stood up and began pacing. She tried to catch his eye each time he passed, but he just looked down. This wasn't the self-assured Grant she had fallen in love with. This was a scared boy who now averted his eyes from her. Ignored her pleas. Ran out the door without a word.

Chapter 5

Their flesh will rot while they are still standing
on their feet, their eyes will rot in their sockets,
and their tongues will rot in their mouths.
    – Zechariah 14:12.

When Grant hadn't returned for half an hour, Stacey took an Uber to Logan Airport. The car was jacked up, the engine loud. The driver, a young guy with a shaved head, said he was just out of rehab.

"Welcome to the club," Stacey sighed.

She drove from Topeka-Jehovah International airport right to her mother's house in Cosgrove, forty miles south. She had tried to block Grant out of her mind all during the trip home. She was now just the latest entry on his Zip-list of women he was through with. What had made her think she was more to him than that? The familiar old feelings of humiliation and worthlessness had set in again. She still had to deal with her brother's legal troubles and her family's dysfunction. And she was going to have a baby – in Kansas.

Stacey now wished she had listened to her mother's complaints about the Certainty Party over the last several months. She had told her mother each time she wasn't interested in criminal law or family law. The real effects of Conception Control hadn't hit her until her experience at the airport. And Feto-Terrorism had seemed like a silly, unenforceable rule until Kendrick's computer was seized. Her mother's vituperation today was aimed mostly at Baldwin Touhey, their own state delegate from Cosgrove.

"He's CP?"

Audrey gave Stacey a look of exasperation. Stacey recognized in her mother's looks – her still-thick chestnut hair pulled back in a loose bun, her oval, delicate face lined only faintly, her dramatic brown eyes now showing as much fear as curiosity, her full lips seemingly trembling between a kiss and a curse – the face she hoped she would not have in twenty-five years.

"Yes, he's CP now. You didn't know that?"

"I'm sorry, Mom. I haven't kept up."

"This is not a joke, Stacey. Reverend Ezekial has been receiving the word of God directly, he says. He tells CP what God says. They enact it into law. It's mostly about putting women under control."

"So Touhey's religious? I knew he ran an insurance agency, but ...."

"*Used to* run an insurance agency. His ex-wife owns it now, after it came out in the divorce that he was messing with the teenage babysitter. He's remarried now. To the babysitter. She's nineteen. They never could prove he did anything to her before she reached the legal age."

Stacey pictured their insurance agent as she had last seen him several years ago, with his oversized bald head, hairless jowls and creepily mobile black eyebrows. "Let me guess. CP is changing the legal age for marriage for women now."

"They're trying. Fourteen."

"Mom, how did you ever even think of getting involved with that stinker, Touhey?"

"Oh, honey, I was young. Teenagers make mistakes."

*** ***

Kendrick had been arrested and charged with Feto-Terrorism. With the help of their new lawyer, Harshaw, Audrey had already got him released on bail. As soon as Stacey brought up Kendrick's case, Audrey's hands would start shaking. Her mother had once been the smart one, the level headed one, the one who went to two years of college and who liked to talk about larger issues than hunting, farming and the Jayhawks.

But she hadn't succeeded in interesting any of her children in politics or economics or psychology or medicine or science. All her talk about a wider world had seemed phony to Stacey when she was in high school. Her mother was a personnel administrator in a real estate firm, and what she actually did was spend her entire day hassling with employees about sick pay, leaves of absence, grievances and other boring things teenage Stacey hadn't wanted to hear about. At home her mother tried to interest her kids in the fascinating, complicated world she assured them was out there – somewhere. It seemed like she had learned just enough in college to be dissatisfied with the normal life she came back to.

"Mom, have you talked to Dad?"

"He knows. He had to sign the papers to put our house up for Kendrick's bail. Amy tracked him down for me." Her father's slow change from steady father and ace machinist to opioid addict had affected her mother the most. Stacey's sure-handed and practical mother with intellectual stars in her eyes had gradually changed into this anxious hand-wringer who stood before her now.

"Mom, it's a good thing that there has to be both of your signatures to put a lien on the house. Having our house in tenancy by the entireties saved our house before. You know Dad would have sold the house out from under us back then if he could have sold it by himself."

"Oh, honey, I don't know that."

"Yes, you do, Mom."

"Let's not fight about that now. Do you want to see Kendrick? Maybe he'll talk to you."

"Is he in his room?"

"Yeah. But honey, the lawyer said not to talk to him about … *that*."

She knocked on his closed bedroom door and waited until

he called out. There was a strong, gamy, boy-smell in the room. He was watching TV with his arm around Shelbie, their aging golden lab. There was some dog smell, too. Kendrick wasn't allowed to touch a computer now. Stacey was ten years older than her brother. She had adored him ever since he was a baby, and she liked to think he looked up to her. He had cried when she went away to college.

"So, what's this movie about?" she began.

Her gambit worked. He did her the tremendous honor of actually turning his head away from the screen and nodding to her. "Zombies."

"There's a lot of zombie shows on now, aren't there?"

"This one's the best. The zombies sneak in your house at night and suck out your blood with needles. But they die easy with one shot to the face. Blam! Got one!"

She stood and waited until the show was over. "Give me a hug!" She was shocked when he stood up. When did he get taller than her? Skinny body, long, even skinnier arms, bright blonde hair, green eyes, he held her in a stiff, formal hug until she pulled him strongly in. Then she let him go. After all, he was becoming a man.

"How are you? With all this crap going down, I mean."

He sat sideways on his chair while she sat on the bed. "You know it all. I was busted. They put me in a cell by myself. Nothing to do but stare at the wall. A toilet with no seat on it. Anybody walks by can see you doing your stuff."

"You were in there for twelve hours?"

"Twenty years. They say 20 years is the minimum if I'm found guilty. All I did was …."

"I can't talk to you about what you did," she interrupted him. Kendrick stood up and walked to the door and back, shaking his arms in frustration. "I'm sorry," she continued, "but anything you say, anything, can get you in even bigger trouble."

"Oh God." He collapsed and lay back on the bed next to her, his eyes closed and his arms stretched up over his head. His shirt pulled up, exposing his bony ribs and almost nonexistent stomach. She cringed at the thought of what the other inmates might do to that scrawny young body in jail. He opened his eyes and sought out hers. "I thought you were almost like a lawyer."

Kendrick's eyes were pleading. There had to be something she could do.

"I'll figure out some way I can help."

"Really, there's not that much to say. It's just ...."

"*Don't*. Not now. I'll do everything I can to protect you. But right now, the best thing you can do is say nothing, absolutely nothing to anyone but your lawyer."

"Ohhhh-kay. You know, you sound like him." His head was lolling back over the edge of the bed like he had done all the straight line thinking he could for the moment. He stuck out his arm and tousled Shelbie's hair. Stacey reached over and tickled Kendrick's stomach.

"Yeow!" He snapped upright so fast his face crashed into her shoulder. He grabbed her hand and pulled it off his stomach. But he held it for a second before he let it go.

"So what's new? Do you still play Black Panther?"

"That's so lame."

"You still hanging around with Jeremy and Pete?"

"Yeah, kind of."

"Are you all going to Cosgrove High in September?"

"Yeah."

"You going to play baseball there?"

"Guess so."

She ran out of things to say. She'd never really known a fourteen-year-old boy before, and now her little brother had turned into one of those mysterious creatures.

"Yeah. Jeremy's sort of got a girlfriend."

"Oh. What's her name?

"Corinne."

"What's she like?"

"She's okay."

"So, do you like any girls?"

"Come on, Stace. Leave me alone."

She left Kendrick watching another zombie show. Regular citizens were organizing, arming, going from house to house blasting the zombies with shotguns. But the zombie population was still growing. There was one in almost every house.

Chapter 6

Stacey drove back to Topeka to interview at Packer, Packer and Doe late that afternoon. She felt she aced the interview. She didn't tell them she was pregnant, but she did have to excuse herself early in the interview to go and quietly throw up in the toilet in the lavender scented restroom. When she came out of the stall, one of the women who was interviewing her was standing at the sink. She asked Stacey if she was all right. Stacey made up a story about something she had eaten on the plane. The woman looked more skeptical than concerned. Of course, in Massachusetts they couldn't have even asked, even if she were eight months pregnant and carrying what looked like a basketball in her stomach. But in Kansas, the law firm partners might think twice before giving an internship to a potential human bomb that might go off and distract an intern from the fourteen-hour-a-day grind expected of her.

She wouldn't be showing when she arrived in late summer for the beginning of her internship. But it was supposed to be a nine-month internship. She had no idea what she would do when things became obvious. She wanted to do what she could to resist the Certainty Party's plans for the women of Kansas, but she wasn't really in a position to call attention to herself. Raising a political fuss wasn't the kind of thing a PPD lawyer would do. Especially a pregnant one. She was sure that by the time things became obvious in the spring they would appreciate her work ethic and intelligence – but would that be enough?

PPD was the go-to firm for legal representation of the regional gas and oil and agribusiness interests. When they weren't engaged in legal battles, they were preparing for them – constant battles to keep their clients' businesses running straight and profitable. That meant constantly fighting off corporate raiders and hostile takeover attempts and shareholder lawsuits and employee claims and government regulators – but, of course, every battle just meant more profit for the firm.

John Packer, one of the three principal partners, had once explained their business plan very candidly to a group of law students. He had just been honored by being inducted into the law school's Alumni Hall of Fame and had taken a few drinks at the banquet table with the dean afterwards. A few students hung around, waiting for the dean to leave to see if they could glean a few words of wisdom from the famous lawyer's lips.

"Law is just the greatest business," the dark and handsome forty-year-old swirled his Old Fashioned and smiled at his would-be acolytes. "Just compare us to our oil clients. They spend weeks, and millions, digging a well. Employees work their asses off on this dangerous job; it's not unusual for workers to get injured. If they hit oil, they might make some money and might not, depending on expenses and how big the hit is and the current price of crude and how well they exploit the field. Otherwise, all they have is a dry hole in the ground.

"Compare that to Packer, Packer and Doe. At PPD, every case is a no-lose situation, especially in the regulatory area. We lobby personally for our oil clients in Topeka and Washington. We organize advocacy groups against any type of proposed regulation that pops up. All on our client's dime. If we win, our clients think we're geniuses. If we lose … well, they still need somebody to explain the new regulations to them, train their personnel, write their manuals, fight all the little battles with the government about exactly how the regulations will be implemented. All on our client's dime, again. So the truth is, when we lose, we probably make even more money than when we win. It's a great business. There's no such thing as a dry hole at PPD."

Although John Packer had made sure there were no recordings made of his conversation, rumors about his informal talk with the students started to spread. Among the law students, his firm became known as Packer, Packer and Dough. John Packer became Dry Hole.

John Packer even dropped in on Stacey's interview. This was a rare honor, and the two female associates who were interviewing her, and the representative of the firm's personnel department, became visibly nervous. But Stacey had to stifle a smile. She knew he was primarily interested in how much money the firm could make from her free labor. So she sped up her presentation, mentioned the law review note she had authored about the policy changes taking place at the FCC, joked that she had no hobbies since she had given up horseback riding two years before, told them her boyfriend would be out of state and would not be distracting her. She tried hard to convince John Packer she would be more than happy to work hard and make him a little bit richer.

She held herself together throughout the interview, but after it was over she leaned against a wall in the hallway, exhausted. Her life plan had been so simple a few days before. She turned and straightened her back against the wall. Grant hadn't wanted her, not as his wife, his real wife who was carrying their baby. He wasn't the rock she had imagined him to be. She would have to reinvent herself, again, without him, and with whatever emotional strength she had left.

The door to the offices opened and John Packer came out walking quickly, but he stopped short when he saw her.

"Are you all right?"

"I'm fine. Just tired. It's been a really long day."

He looked like he didn't believe her. "Would you like to step into one of our empty conference rooms? I'll have someone bring you some water. You can rest there."

"I'm okay."

"No, you're not. Come on in. Sit down." He actually took her hand and guided her into an empty conference room, this one also with a panoramic view. They were looking down at the state capital building far below and just across the street. "Just rest for a minute, please." He left but came back trailing an employee who brought a silver pitcher of ice water and placed it on the table. "Just rest for a minute."

She was glad to sit down. He sat down at the far end of the table. Her life was moving too fast. She rubbed her hand along the smooth, polished oak of the conference table and stared down at the city below through the plate glass window. From this height, the buildings seemed small, the people almost indistinguishable, their problems small and manageable.

"I remember you from that chat we all had at the bar, after the alumni presentation," Packer surprised her. "I'm embarrassed that story got around. But I need to talk to you about something else now."

She really was tired. But how could she tell the mighty John Packer she'd rather be alone than chat with him?

"Our firm is in an unusual position. Have you heard about the new CP bill, the Professional Reform Act?"

"What? No."

"If you have time right now, I'd like you to read the bill. He texted his assistant, who brought the bill in and laid it in front of him on the table. She laid another copy in front of Stacey.

Definitions

"Lifelong economic dependent" means a female residing in this region who is pregnant or who is the unwed or widowed or divorced mother of a child ....

Legislative Findings

The legislature finds that the existence of lifelong economic dependents in our educational and training institutions has resulted in:

(a) the removal of professional opportunities from citizens of this state capable of making more productive use of such education or training;

(b) an inordinate strain on the traditional family structure which is the most beneficial for the raising of educated Christian children;

(c) the threat of the reversal of the natural order of domestic relationships revealed in the words of the Holy Bible....

Accordingly, in all public and private institutions in this state:

1. A lifelong economic dependent may not be admitted to, or graduate from:

(a) any institution which grants any post-graduate degree; or

(b) any training program that that requires entrants to have any degree of education higher than secondary school....

This enactment being an emergency measure, it will go into effect immediately upon the signature of the governor or the vote of the legislature to override a veto by the governor, whichever is appropriate....

Stacey read no further. "This ... this *thing*. It isn't *law* yet, is it?" She looked across the table at Packer.

"The Professional Reform Act is just a bill right now," he admitted. "But the Certainty Party has the votes to pass it. This firm is well connected politically. Our sources tell us that, when all is said and done, this will be the law of Kansas."

"This is sickening. Thank you for telling me about this. But why are you telling me now?"

"Packer, Packer and Doe is counsel to the Board of Trustees of the University. If the bill passes, we have to advise them on how to implement the law."

"Oh!" Stacey sat up. She couldn't mask her excitement. "You are thinking of advising the Board of Trustees that the law is unconstitutional? And you're offering me a chance to start researching it as part of my internship?"

"Not exactly." Packer pushed himself back from the table. "In fact, nothing at all like that. An internship at PPD, Miss Davenport, is essentially a training ground for future associates who will work at the firm. We invest a lot of time training the interns, and we hire almost all of our new lawyers from the ranks of those interns."

"I know. That's why I was so pleased ...."

Packer interrupted her. "Ms. Davenport, although your qualifications are excellent, the fact is, the Professional Reform Act is going to pass. I've talked privately with the interview team, and we have reason to believe you are pregnant."

The encounter in the restroom, Stacey suddenly realized, might have been the most important part of the interview.

"Your present condition," Packer continued, "we are convinced, will prevent you from getting your law degree. Without a degree, you will be of no long-term use to us. Therefore, there is no point in PPD investing any time and money in training you. Therefore, we will have to decline your application for an internship here."

He walked her to the elevator. She was too deflated to say anything. The doors closed. As far as PPD was concerned, she was just a dry hole.

Chapter 7

Stacey immediately collapsed on the sofa back in her apartment near the law school in Lawrence. She had never felt so crushed and totally defeated since the day back in high school when she admitted to herself that she could not, absolutely could not, stop taking drugs. She had overcome a lot of obstacles since then, but all that effort was now coming to nothing. As all of her hopes faded away, that old itch rose up inside her again. She knew she could call her old rehab sponsor, but she was too exhausted even to get up. She fell asleep and dreamed that she was wandering around Lawrence, searching desperately for a dealer.

She was awakened by a knock at the apartment door. A persistent, low knock. She hadn't turned on the air conditioning or closed the curtains on the plate-glass door to her balcony, and now the evening sun was pouring through and heating her skin to a sticky sweat. She had to get up. As the dream faded, she had to remind herself she was not supposed to be searching for drugs any more. She roused herself and straightened her clothes but decided she didn't need to look in the mirror or comb her hair.

"Hi, Roland. Come in."

He bounced in, always peppy, always smiling. Stacey thought how easy it must be to feel at ease when every woman you pass takes a second look. "You look tired," he said to her. "Is this a bad time?"

"A bad time for what?"

"Well, you know, Communications Law."

"Oh. Right. Is it that late? I'm a little disoriented. I got back from Boston, drove to my mother's house, drove to my interview at PPD, came back here and just crashed. Come on in. It's nice to see a friendly face."

It was definitely nice to see Roland's face. Any woman would appreciate that shock of slightly tousled blonde hair, those smiling blue eyes, that wide movie star smile. Roland was a little older, maybe 30. He was a law student – and also a state delegate. He had a politician's way of making everybody feel like he was their best friend. He lived with his wife, Frieda, in the apartment right above Stacey's. The building was just a few blocks from campus.

Frieda was also tall and blonde like Roland, but she wasn't nearly so outgoing. She would have been beautiful but for her loose and long back country hairdo, complete with bangs. Stacey admired Frieda's intellect. They had taken Constitutional Law class and studied together in their first year. But Stacey had been dismayed to find out how religiously conservative she was. Frieda believed it was her religious duty to obey her husband Roland in all things. Frieda apparently got this idea from *The Prophet*, Reverend Ezekial's podcast she listened to every day. Stacey admired Frieda's consistency and integrity, but she imagined Frieda would be a hard person to warm up to.

"You look so tired, Stacey," Roland said now. "Why don't I go back upstairs and we just skip Communications Law for the night?" She felt his eyes studying her. "Or, better yet, why don't we walk down to Mario's Pizza and just get something to eat."

"I am hungry."

The owner, Mario, greeted them in person, thanking Roland effusively for some favor he had done.

"You did some political favor for the restaurant?" Stacey inquired.

"Not exactly political. I found an apartment for his daughter. I know a landlord."

Besides being a law student, Roland was a state delegate for Shawnee County, which included Topeka. "Is that what politicians do? Find apartments for people?"

Roland shrugged. His medium-length, stylishly messy blonde hair gently waved in the draft from the air conditioner. His short, dark beard and moustache emphasized his white skin and gorgeous blue eyes. Stacey wondered if he'd ever been a model.

"How'd your trip to Boston go?"

"On the plane, on my way there, I found out the state police seized my little brother's computer. Without a warrant. He's going to be charged under the Feto-Terrorism law. How could you legislators let that law happen?"

"Look, I know. It's awful. My caucus voted against it. Against Conception Control, too. No business is ever going to relocate here if the businessmen's wives are treated like that."

"Who cares about *businesses*? This is women's freedom we're talking about."

"You know, the head of the Certainty Party in the Kansas House of Representatives is your own delegate, Baldwin Touhey."

"What! Touhey!"

"True." At first, he looked surprised she didn't know. But then his smooth politician manners kicked in. "I guess a lot has happened since you left for college in Boston six years ago. And I know how busy you've been with law school the last two years."

"That guy, Touhey, he just married his nineteen-year-old ex-babysitter. I'm going to tell you something you won't believe. My mother used to date him. A long time ago. In high school. They were even sort of informally engaged. She threw him over to go to college."

"Oh. Well, everybody in the legislature knows he married the babysitter, and that he hates his ex-wife. It's not hurting him in Certainty Party circles."

"But why do they have to torture my brother? He's only fourteen years old."

"You're really the head of your family, aren't you?"

She looked up. "I guess you could say that. In a way. I've told you about my mother. I never told you about my father. He's an addict, and really long-term. The story goes on and on. You don't want to hear it all."

"I know you've had a tough row to hoe. You've accomplished a lot under difficult circumstances." He met her eyes momentarily, then glanced aside.

"Thank you, Roland." It felt nice that he noticed. "You know, I've been so self-absorbed, I never asked you much about yourself. I guess I stereotyped you as a typical politician – I mean a good one, but still a politician."

He smiled. Shrugged. "Despite what you hear, politicians are people too. At least some of them." They both smiled at his weak joke. Roland went on. "They have problems too … including domestic problems."

"You and Frieda? The perfect law school power couple?"

But he didn't laugh. Instead, he looked like he was thinking hard about what he should say.

"We're having problems."

Had he just crossed some kind of line? Now it was Stacey's turn to decide if she should go there, maybe cross a line. She had been thoroughly beaten down today. She was tired. The easiest thing was not to make any decision for now, and just play along.

"You mean like, serious difficulties?"

"Possibly," he muttered, then stopped. Stacey stayed quiet, giving him license to say more. Mario interrupted them right then by personally bringing the pizza to the table. Their responses to Mario were very subdued this time. Both of them were now just waiting for him to go away.

Mario retreated to the kitchen. Stacey wasn't going to beg Roland for details of his problems with Frieda. If he wanted to tell her, he would tell her. They each took a bite of their pizza and pretended to be interested in the food. They each took a sip of their drinks.

"I guess you could call it a serious problem," he finally said, leaning toward her, his voice very low. "I've been thinking a lot. Worrying. About something I maybe shouldn't be talking to you about."

She knew he was giving her a chance to stop him. She didn't feel a deep attraction for this man. He was smart, great-looking and nice to her, and his political heart was in the right place, but she wasn't falling in love with him and she wasn't sure she ever would. She felt she knew men now, knew the species. She had experienced how their love could burn bright enough to warm her soul, make her willing to break boundaries – but she also knew it was an evanescent fire, delectable in the moment, but short-lived, and useless in the end.

Chapter 8

Smite the Amaleks and utterly destroy all that they have; do not spare them, but kill both man and woman, child and suckling, ox and sheep, camel and ass. – II Samuel 15:33

The skinny man coming toward her on the sidewalk made eye contact with her, then suddenly stopped and bowed his head. He was old, with receding grey hair, wearing jeans and a T-shirt pulled tight over his expansive pot belly. There was a short, straight, brown mark on his forehead, like a scar. As Stacey came near, he backed completely off the sidewalk onto the street, lowered his eyes and bowed his head even lower. She was pretty sure she didn't know him. He kept standing in the gutter with his head bowed like an abject beggar until she passed by. A chill ran up her spine as she did.

Roland had recommended talking to her state representative in Cosgrove. They are the people who make the laws, and you should tell them what you think, he told her. Her mother and Touhey had reached some kind of truce after she quit college after two years, returned to Cosgrove – and married somebody else, Stacey's father, Don. As part of the unspoken truce with Touhey, her mother had even used his insurance agency. But she had no use for Touhey after he married the babysitter. Roland had encouraged Stacey to meet with him anyway and let him know how angry she was about Conception Control and Feto-Terrorism and the proposed Professional Reform Act. She smirked as she passed the sign announcing the Touhey Insurance Office. His wife got that in the divorce and hadn't changed the name, probably just to twist the knife a little more. His legislative office was in a converted frame house across the street that he shared with two dentists and a veterinarian.

"Miss Davenport, Stacey. My, you've grown! You look just like your mother did at your age." Touhey had not aged well since Stacey had last seen him. The skin on his bald, bullet head was sagging and creased, and his dark eyebrows wavered even more erratically as he spoke. His belly was growing. He should have had enough sense not to wear a white shirt. He was obviously slowing down. She wondered how his nineteen-year-old wife was taking that.

"If your Professional Reform Act passes, I'll be kicked out of law school, in my last year."

"The Certainty Party, as guided by Reverend Ezekial, is enacting God's law, as written in the Holy Bible, as the law of the land."

"My fourteen-year-old brother, who's never been out of Cosgrove and has never even had a girlfriend, is charged with Feto-Terrorism. No pregnant woman can travel out of state, even to go on vacation, because of Conception Control."

"Women should stay home when they're pregnant."

"Who says?"

"God says. The Bible says. Reverend Ezekial says. And we are only just beginning to transform this state into a Kingdom of God on earth." He was smiling, almost smirking at her. Touhey was clearly looking forward to this new kingdom. "And it's all according to the Bible."

"What part of the Bible?"

"All of it."

"Smite the Amaleks? Kill all the men, women and children?"

"There are no Amaleks now, of course." Touhey brought his giant eyebrows together in a frown. "We will have to seek the guidance of Reverend Ezekial to see if those words refer to any specific group today."

"So you think there may be groups that need to be annihilated?"

Touhey smiled at her alarm. "Let's say we're making some

progress. Not annihilation at this time. But submission to God's will, by force if necessary."

Too shocked to respond, Stacey stood up to go. As she reached the doorway, Touhey added in a more conciliatory tone, "You should join with us. Reverend Ezekial's businesses are expanding, and he could use a smart young woman like you. You should get in on the ground floor."

"I don't think so."

"Before it's too late."

On the way back to her mother's house from Touhey's office, Stacey saw the same man with the mark on his face. He was carrying what looked like a bag of groceries. Every time he met someone coming the other way, he backed off the curb, stepped into the gutter, and bowed his head. Cosgrove was starting to seem like another world.

*** ***

Stacey didn't have to tell her mother about Touhey's political beliefs. Her mother already knew more than she did. "Didn't he tell you he also thinks men should be able to have more than one wife?"

"Mom, this whole thing is scary. If the Professional Reform Act passes, women will be forced out of the professions. If the Certainty Party gets away with that, they'll go further. Women will become so dependent on men they'll have no lives of their own."

"I think that's what Touhey wants. His first wife, Eileen, was always the boss in their household, you know. I'm just thinking that man must have been sitting up in his little insurance office dreaming up revenge fantasies his whole life."

"Maybe his revenge is about you, too. You threw him over to go to college, right?"

Audrey smiled. "Yeah. That was one good decision I made.

Then, two years later, I made a terrible decision and dropped out of college to marry your Dad."

"That wasn't a terrible decision, Mom. Don't think that. Dad loved us. I'm sure. He would still help us if he could. He wasn't as bad as you think."

"Hm." Her mother signaled that she had heard as much talk about her father as she could stand for the moment.

"Mom, the strangest thing happened out on the sidewalk today. There was this man who kept stepping back into the gutter and bowing his head whenever anybody passed by."

"Mark on his forehead?"

"Yes. You know him?"

"No, but I wouldn't worry about it. There's a lot of them. He's just a marko."

"What's a *marko*?"

"Another new law they passed. Only applies to repeat felony offenders. They get branded. Can't vote, can't drive, can't be out at night, can't take any job a regular person wants, can't be on the sidewalk at the same time as a non-marko, must always move back to be the last in line. Anyway, your uncle Randy, the sheriff, doesn't enforce any of that crap in Cosgrove County. I guess the guy you saw was afraid somebody would complain anyway."

Chapter 9

Losing the PPD internship put a big dent in Stacey's career plans, but she still hoped to get her law degree, and she didn't have to have that particular PPD internship to graduate. She did need some type of internship, though. Staying at her mother's house in Cosgrove City for a few days, watching Audrey and Amy and Kendrick not talk to each other on the orders of their lawyer, Harshaw, she got an idea. Three weeks before, she would have thought it laughable to become the intern of this rumpled, plump, small-town criminal and divorce lawyer, but now Harshaw was the perfect solution. Harshaw was surprised at her suggestion, but not unhappy, and he agreed. That meant, as his intern, and part of Harshaw's law firm, she was technically Kendrick's lawyer, too. As his lawyer, she could talk to her brother about his case, and nothing he said would be revealed to the police or the prosecutor. She could also talk to her mother, to Amy, and to her father.

"Blam! Blam!"

Kendrick was sitting on his bed playing a video game. Zombies were stalking the streets in ultra-slow motion. No one was safe from being changed into one. A family watching television in their living room with their teenage daughter were slowly realizing that she had turned.

"Blam! Blam!"

Stacey could understand Kendrick's satisfaction in blasting these soulless monsters from the screen. But she knew what it was like to feel soulless. She often had to push back those memories of her relentless, single-minded scrabbling for drugs, scenes that played back in her head when she least expected them. She prayed she would never give in to those urges again. But she had to focus on Kendrick now. She could maybe even help Kendrick now.

She didn't bother saying hi. "Where did you get that game? I thought they took all electronic stuff away from you."

"Dad brought it to me." Kendrick didn't say hi either.

"*Dad* brought it to you? When did Dad come here?"

"He comes here all the time at night."

Stacey didn't understand why this news made her so uncomfortable. "How? His hideout room is 25 miles west of here in Neola County. He doesn't even have a driver's license. And he's not allowed out at night." She strained to keep herself from shouting.

"Dunno. He has some kind of motorcycle he made."

"Does Mom know about this?'

"Dunno."

Stacey couldn't think about this now. She was the only one who could talk to Kendrick about his case. She had to do it now. She reached in and turned off the video game. He pointed the controller at her.

"Blam!"

"Kendrick, what did you actually do on the computer in the last few weeks before the police took it away?"

"I'm not supposed to say anything."

"I know, but I'm working for Jason Harshaw now, and …."

"Who?"

"Your lawyer. He's representing you in your case. I'm working with him now. So you can talk to me. I'm your lawyer too, for now."

"Okay. Awesome!" He gave Stacey the biggest smile she'd seen from him in months.

She couldn't help herself when she saw that goofy smile. She jumped on his bed and started tickling him.

"Stop. Stop. Sis, I'm too old for this. I mean, really. Stop!"

She stopped. "Sorry. I won't do that any more. You are too old for that. It's inappropriate lawyer conduct anyway. So. Let's talk. Tell me what you did. Remember, I can't tell anyone, not even Mom."

"It was Jeremy. I mean his girlfriend. Corinne. She was pregnant. Or she thought she was. I don't know." He was lying back now, looking at the ceiling, his voice flat.

"What do you mean, you don't know?"

"She wanted me to look up all this creepy stuff on the internet. You know, fetuses and stuff. But now I don't think she was pregnant."

"Why don't you think she was?"

"I don't know. She's not … getting fat, you know? And it's been a long time."

"But what does she say?"

"She doesn't talk to me. Nobody talks to me."

Stacey was due back at school in Lawrence in two and a half hours. "Under the new law, terrorism includes helping anyone get an abortion, go out of state to get an abortion, or supplying information about abortion or any related procedure."

"Guilty."

"Guilty of what?"

"The supplying information thing. She knew Conception Control checks every internet search every girl over the age of twelve makes. She thought they wouldn't check me so much."

"So you helped her? How'd you do it?"

"We just googled it. You know, looked in states where you can do all kinds of shit."

"Did you print anything out?"

He looked at her like she was crazy.

"Okay," she said. "Did you forward any information to her phone – or to anybody?"

"No, we just looked on my computer a couple hours one day. That's it."

"What does Jeremy say about getting her pregnant?"

"I told you nobody talks to me."

Stacey got Harshaw on the phone on her way back to

school.

"I've talked to my brother. This seems like the most minimal offense I can imagine. Is this really terrorism?"

"That's what the new law says it is." Because of Harshaw's appearance, Stacey had been suspicious that he was lazy and would be a sloppy lawyer. This was a kind of prejudice she couldn't even speak out loud in Massachusetts, but she allowed herself to think this in Kansas. She knew Harshaw was the key to allowing her to speak to Kendrick, and she knew he could take away that privilege at any time, so she curbed her skepticism.

"It's a stupid, vicious law."

"I know, but that's irrelevant now. It is the law, and our job is to see that it doesn't come down on Kendrick any harder than it has to."

"I know. But I'm his sister too, and I have to do something about getting this law changed. I just … I guess I'm warning you, Mr. Harshaw. I'm going to make a big fuss about this law, somehow."

"Call me Jason, Stacey. Can I call you Stacey? Stacey." He sounded like he was practicing the name. "Stacey, the prosecutor has a lot of discretion in a case like this. If things get too ugly, I mean politically speaking, they could always come down really hard on Kendrick. You wouldn't want that."

"Got it. But Jason, I have to do what I have to do. These CP people are quickly turning Kansas into a totalitarian state. It seems like everybody is afraid to speak out. I have to do something. I'm asking you to let me stay on Kendrick's case, too. I need to be able to talk to my family."

She heard him sigh. "Well, it might complicate things. For you to stay as his attorney, I mean." There was a long pause on the line. "Well, okay, Stacey. Let's just play it by ear, see where it goes."

"Thank you, Jason."

Chapter 10

"You have to get down here." Harshaw's voice, normally a lazy, gravelly bass, had an edge. She was in her apartment in Lawrence and was just finishing up the paperwork to have her internship with Harshaw accepted for credit at the school. "Kendrick's bail has been revoked. He's entitled to a hearing on his detention pending trial. But he won't talk to me. And that girl, Corinne, won't talk to me either."

She went to Harshaw's office as soon as she arrived back in Cosgrove. Harshaw walked out of another meeting to update her on Kendrick's case. "The prosecutor's running scared on these Feto-Terrorism cases. Reverend Ezekial is criticizing him day and night about lax enforcement. He's found some reason to revoke Kendrick's bail. Something about his being a danger to the other students at school."

"Oh my God."

"Your uncle, Sheriff Randy Crenshaw, convinced them to detain him here. The hearing's here, tomorrow, in Cosgrove Circuit Court. But I can't get anything out of Kendrick at all."

"You've already been over to the jail?"

"Twice."

Stacey was impressed. Harshaw was not lazy. "Maybe he'll talk to me."

"What about that girl?"

"Corinne? I'll try her, too."

The jail was in the same building as Randy's office. Stacey talked to Randy first.

"Did Kendrick make any new statements to the KBI?"

"Not that I know of. They said he was real quiet."

"Did he make any statements to you?"

"No. I'm kin. I couldn't interrogate him anyway."

Stacey arranged for Kendrick to talk to her. He was in his

cell, wearing a bright orange jumpsuit. Kendrick stuck his hands out to be shackled without looking up at her. He walked slowly with his head down into the interrogation room and sat down without making eye contact with his sister.

"I'm really sorry this happened," she started. When he didn't respond or even look up, she went on. "If you'll try to help me out, I think I can get you released on bail again until your trial."

"I don't care."

He was looking straight down at the steel surface of the table. Seeing her little brother slumped down and manacled in front of her like a convicted murderer, she had to choke back a sob. She put her hands on both of his manacled wrists and took a deep breath. But he didn't seem to need or want her sympathy right then; she knew what he needed now was her brains.

"Did you tell the state police anything?" Her voice came out narrow, strangled by the effort to say only what needed to be said.

"No. Like you told me. Even though they yelled at me for like an hour."

"Did you tell anybody anything about this at school – I mean in the last couple of days?"

"No. Nobody would listen to me anyway. They were all trashing me – except my crew."

"Okay. Um, what's a crew?"

"Three or four guys. Friends. I don't talk about this to them either. You told me not to."

"So you do have friends. I thought you told me before nobody would talk to you at all. Because you said nobody wanted to be associated with a terrorist."

"They do talk. They talk *about* me."

"Can't you just ignore it? I told you, you should probably not look at any social media at all."

"Not social media. Nobody does that any more. You might as well talk directly to the KBI, or Conception Control. But, you know, kids actually talk. Yell. In the halls, outside, on the street, everywhere. And these cards."

"Cards?"

"You know, like playing cards, but with pictures of terrorists. Including me. And Corinne. *The slut card.*"

"Who's doing this? Do you know who's behind it? Because I can talk to the principal."

"It's not the kids. It's the motorcycle guys. Everybody's scared of them. One of them broke up Amy's circle."

*** ***

"Any argument on behalf of the detainee?" the judge intoned.

Richard Cory, the prosecutor, had just presented what he stated were compelling reasons why Kendrick's bail should be revoked pending his trial on terrorism charges. Kendrick was supposedly not only a budding feto-terrorist but also the leader of a gang publicly blaspheming and inciting resistance to the new laws in Kansas.

Harshaw was the real lawyer who would argue on behalf of Kendrick to the judge. Stacey, as the legal intern, was permitted to sit at the counsel table with him. Kendrick sat between them in his orange jump suit, his wrists and ankles still manacled. A sheriff's deputy sat behind him.

"What is he talking about?" Stacey whispered urgently to Kendrick. "What gang?"

"Dunno." Kendrick seemed truly clueless. "Maybe my crew?"

"Your Honor," the prosecutor went on, "the Kansas Bureau of Investigation has produced a transcript of some of his downloads. I'm not going to repeat in open court the blasphemous and obscene words he wrote, but let me just state that this kind of incitement to rebellion is a threat to the life, health and safety of the ordinary schoolchildren who are subject to it."

Harshaw jumped up and interrupted. "Your Honor, I would like to see those transcripts the prosecutor has been describing."

The prosecutor glared at him. "Sure. Here. Now, if I can just sum up without being interrupted again, I can't think of a more compelling case for continued detention. We have a presumed terrorist here, under charges so serious he may well feel that he has nothing to lose, encouraging others to resist the laws in his vicious, obscene, violent postings. And as we all know, he is fourteen years old and has the absolute right to bear arms, even in his situation."

"Let's start with 'presumed terrorist,'" lawyer Harshaw began. "'Presumed terrorist.' That's an error of law right off the bat. I believe I learned in my first year of law school that an accused is presumed innocent until proven guilty. I don't think even the current Kansas legislature has revoked that principle yet."

"Fair enough. I'll ignore that, counsel. The defendant is presumed innocent of terrorism."

"And there's not a speck of evidence that he carries, or even owns, a firearm."

"Fair enough," the judge interrupted. "But let's talk about the main reason we're here today. Your client is charged with a crime that could result in 20 years to life in prison. That's incentive enough to flee. And the prosecutor says there's now evidence he's becoming unhinged and is inciting violence. This frankly scares me. And anyone over the age of fourteen can carry a gun in this state. So I'm thinking, would he now pose a threat to the community if I let him out on bail again? Can you speak on those issues?"

Harshaw paused, sighed, glanced at the paper in his hand and passed it over to Stacey. Stacey looked at it. At first, she cringed, but then she stared at the paper longer, then turned and whispered excitedly to Harshaw. Harshaw stared back at her for a long time, and she nodded her head, again, and again. Finally, Harshaw turned back to the judge.

"Your Honor, we would like you to see these writings."

"No problem at all with that, Your Honor," Cory the prosecutor smirked.

The judge actually made faces as he silently read the words Kendrick had written. Then he seemed to start reading all over from the beginning. Then he stopped, shook his head, rolled his eyes. Then he turned to the prosecutor. "Haven't you ever heard of rap?"

The judge ordered Kendrick released again, and with the same amount of bail that Audrey had already posted.

Harshaw looked at Stacey with a question mark in his eyes. "How did you know …?"

"I researched the judge," she whispered. "He's got five teenage kids."

But the judge wasn't finished. "I am concerned, however, about the risk of flight. Therefore, I am ordering that the bail be contingent on the defendant wearing an electronic ankle brace-let that can track his location in real time, that the defendant must attend school regularly, and that the defendant remain at his mother's house at all times that he isn't in school."

Stacey got Kendrick to walk downtown with her from the courthouse. She wanted to take him to a fast food place or to the video arcade – for his last taste of freedom of movement until his trial. Anything to get him to talk to her. But they didn't have much of a chance to talk.

Moving away from the manicured lawn of the courthouse, crossing the tiny, tree-lined park that was at the center of the Cosgrove town square, they turned the corner onto Greyson Street, the main business thoroughfare. They immediately saw a crowd spilling onto the street. People were gathered in a circle, yelling and screaming. Two motorcycles in the middle of the crowd were snarling angrily, then going into crescendos of ear-splitting revs. Stacey backed up against a store window and tried to pull Kendrick with her. But he pulled away from her and ran to the edge of the crowd.

"It's them!" He yelled at her when he came back. "The vigilantes!"

"Stay back here! I'm calling Randy." But he ran off. Stacey couldn't get Randy, or even the sheriff's office, on the phone. She heard a scream from the middle of the crowd and tiptoed forward to see what she could see. Kendrick came back.

"You got to see what they're doing!"

"Who's screaming? I can't see anything."

"Here. Get on my shoulders."

Really? Skinny little Kendrick? But the screaming and shouting got worse, and she had to see. Kendrick stooped down and she got on his shoulders, and with unbelievable teenage strength Kendrick lifted her up and she swayed over the crowd until she could see what was happening.

It was the grey-haired man she had seen the day before, the one her mother called a marko. He was on the ground between the two motorcycles. A figure in a black motorcycle jacket and a ski mask was kicking him. Another masked motorcyclist walked slowly around the scene swinging a heavy chain, keeping the crowd away.

People in the crowd were yelling. "Stop that! Stop that!" "We're calling 911." "The sheriff will be here soon!" But no one dared go near the swinging chain. Stacey saw the marko get halfway up. The attacker kicked him again. He fell into the motorcycle, screaming as his arm was burned on the exhaust pipes. Both men laughed. Stacey looked for the license numbers, but the plates on the motorcycles were covered with black tape.

The beating went on. One of the Riders was using a chain now. Stacey felt sick. She pleaded for Kendrick to let her down.

Then, finally, police sirens could be heard approaching. Both men jumped on their motorcycles and roared away, both giving the finger to the approaching cars.

* * * * * *

Stacey had never seen her uncle Randy at work enforcing the law before. And she'd never seen him look so pissed. No one at the scene could give him a good description of either of the men. There wasn't likely any blood at the scene other than the marko's. Nobody could describe the motorcycles except Kendrick, and all he knew was one was a Harley. Two patrol cars had given chase, and the state police were setting up roadblocks up ahead, but Randy didn't think they'd find them. Stacey heard him call and ask for a helicopter.

"Is this another marko assault?" the voice on the line said.

"Yeah. Looks like the guy might die."

"We'll see what we can do."

"That means they're not going to any trouble," Randy confided to Stacey after he clicked off. "State police are discouraged. Governor Adams pardoned one of those motorcycle militiamen for beating up a protestor."

Chapter 11

Stacey knew there was only one reason they might let her in. "I'm Kendrick's sister," she told Corinne's mother at the door. "I'd really like to talk to Corinne, if you don't mind."

She knew it would work. This was Kansas. People were nice. Family was important.

"Oh. Okay. I'll get her. You can sit on the davenport in here." Stacey sank into the plush sofa cushions and waited while Corinne's mother ran upstairs. Stacey would rather talk to Corinne in her room, alone, but she had to make do. This was her only chance. When Corinne appeared, Stacey braced herself, then asked Corinne's mother to leave. Corinne's mother nodded, paused, and left the room, looking a little disappointed. Corinne was dressed in jeans and a tank top. She was short, thin, with thick blonde hair, pretty green eyes and a steep triangle of a face. There was something between a smile and a grimace on her lips. She had not been charged with any crime yet, probably because the IP address for all of the suspect computer searches was Kendrick's laptop.

Kendrick had refused to tell the police who he was doing the search for. The cops had then pulled Corinne in for questioning, but her mother, incensed that the government was enacting into law every one of Reverend Ezekial's misogynous daydreams, had gone in to the police station with her and told her not to say "one fucking word." Although a lot of other amendments had been gutted by the Supreme Court in recent years, the Fifth Amendment still mostly applied. They could threaten her, but they could not force her to talk.

"Look, Corinne," Stacey said, once Corinne's mother had grudgingly turned and walked out of the room, "I'm his sister, but I'm also his lawyer."

"Oh."

"Kendrick is charged with a serious crime."

"Feto-Terrorism?"

"Yeah. They changed the law last year. Procuring an abortion, or aiding a person in finding an abortion, and a whole list of other things relating to fetuses, is now considered terrorism. He can go to jail for 20 years to life. Look, I know Kendrick. I don't think he can take the pressure. I'm afraid. I'm afraid he'd kill himself first."

"He didn't really do anything." Corrine mumbled, her thin lips turned down in anger. Stacey was glad to see that. She wanted her angry.

"That's what I hope to show in court. It's the police who have to prove he did something wrong. They know he was looking at some websites. But they can't prove why." Corinne looked like she wanted to say something, but Stacey put up her hand. She knew this conversation could determine the course of the rest of Kendrick's life. In certain situations, there's only so much a lawyer wants to know. "Obviously," she went on, "he wasn't searching abortion websites for himself." She looked directly into Corinne's eyes.

"Corinne, nothing you say to me will get back to the police or will be used against him. If you know something that can help him …."

"Okay."

"So, the police know that the websites were reached from Kendrick's computer. They know that you visited his house sometime that week. People can put two and two together, but that's different from proving it in a court of law."

"I was just …."

"Wait a minute! Let me finish first. Then, if you don't mind, I'm going to ask you some questions, and for now, just for now, could you just answer those questions, *only*?"

Corinne nodded okay, her impossibly thick hair framing her impossibly thin face. Her lips compressed into a thin line as she clamped her jaw shut, forcing herself to wait for Stacey to go on.

"In order for them to prove he's guilty, they have to prove: first, that he searched these websites; second, that he did it on behalf of someone who was pregnant; and third, that his intent was to help someone obtain information about an abortion."

"I don't want him to lose his life just because he …."

"Hold it!"

"I like him!" Corrine shouted.

"Hold on. It really would be better if you let me control this."

But Stacey felt optimistic. Corinne seemed to be catching on. How much was she willing to say? At whose risk?

"I get it." Corrine looked up suddenly at Stacey, her green eyes flaring. "I get it. I'm not stupid."

*** ***

In the movie scene Amy was watching, a dark and very handsome young man had just shown his vampire teeth to the camera as he caressed his teenage girlfriend. Amy didn't turn it off when Stacey entered her room without knocking.

"How's it going?"

Amy ignored her, but then reached over and tried to slide the bedspread over the top of a cardboard box on the floor.

"What's that smell? Bananas?"

"Ripe bananas."

"What? You didn't deliver the food to Dad!"

Amy sighed, turned down the sound a little, but kept her face toward the screen. "I tried, but last time there was this creepy guy hanging around. I got scared."

"You got scared, and so you left Dad with no food?"

"He can get his own food now, I guess."

This limp teenager lying on the bed staring at the screen with her head propped on her elbows wasn't the spunky little sister Stacey had grown up with. Stacey jumped down hard next to her on the bed, bouncing Amy off her elbows in the process.

"Cut it out, Stacey."

"You've been sitting in your room not talking to anybody for three days, Mom says. She's afraid you're doing drugs."

"Mom doesn't know *anything*."

No, she really doesn't, Stacey thought. She didn't know *I* was doing drugs. Her mother's idea of what her children were doing had always been created out of a mixture of anxiety and wishful thinking. At least Stacey had had her father as a bad example. Amy had nobody.

"Amy, you probably didn't notice back then. You were little. But I was really depressed. Look, I know what it's like. I mean, I was more than depressed." Stacey steeled herself for Amy's reaction to what she was going to say. "I was a really bad heroin addict when I was your age."

"Sure. Right. Perfect Stacey was a heroin addict. Give me a break."

It actually felt good to break the big-sister myth. There was a lot she needed to tell Amy. "It was all covered up. You were too little to notice. It was really bad, Amy. Remember that summer when we were going to go to Disney World, but Mom sent me to Aunt Ellen's farm for that fancy equestrian camp instead?"

Amy glanced up at the framed picture of Foxie, the chestnut mare the family used to own. Years ago, she had stolen the picture from Stacey's room and put it on her wall.

"Yeah. We never made it to Disney World."

"Well, there wasn't any equestrian camp. That was just a story Mom and Dad made up. To protect me. It was a drug rehab center in Wisconsin. That was the first time I got clean."

Amy's mouth dropped open. "We never went on a vacation after that. I always thought, you know, it didn't matter. You and Dad were gone anyway."

"I guess I soaked up a lot of the family savings. But Dad used up even more."

"You two were doing drugs together?"

"No. No. No. He was first. It made me so sad. That's why I started. At least that's what I told myself. That was my excuse. But everybody's got some kind of excuse."

"It's not drugs." Amy lay back on the bed, her long, light brown hair falling in straight bangs across her forehead, her full lips compressed in silence.

"What is it?"

"It's everything. The way things are. You have no idea."

"I know it's scary, what's going on. Kendrick and I just saw two motorcycle guys kick a man half to death on the street. And the state police won't help Randy go after them."

"Why did they beat up the guy in the street?"

"It's this thing the government does to released felons now. They put like, this brand or mark on their forehead. It's like, to show everybody you're not a full-fledged human being."

"I know about that."

"Well, they beat this guy up just because he had that mark. That's what everybody on the street said."

"I heard they're marking drug addicts, too, now," Amy said.

"What? Oh my God! That's horrible. I'm just thinking, what if they marked Dad? People with that mark, they treat them like they're *subhumans*."

"Dad says they'll never catch him."

"Since when do you talk to Dad?"

"He's been coming here lately, at night. He talks to me sometimes."

"Jesus Christ, Amy! Am I the only one in this family that doesn't know what's going on?"

"I'm not supposed to tell you." Amy sighed. "He comes after dark when they can't catch him on the roads. Mom won't let him in the house. He's different now. I guess he's different. I don't remember him too much from when I was little."

Stacey grabbed her sister's hand. "Amy, I really think there is some hope. We can fight back against these maniacs running our state. There is this one guy, a law student I know who's also a legislator, who might help. We're going to do something, I don't know exactly what. We're going to try to make sure this craziness and hate won't affect you, or your friends. And that you'll be safe."

Amy pulled her hand away. For the first time in their conversation, Amy looked her sister right in the eye. Then, mouth pursed tightly and dramatic brown eyes wide open and staring, she moved her bangs aside so her sister could clearly see the brand on her forehead.

Chapter 12

"I'll tell my sorry tale if you'll tell me yours." Roland shook his head sadly.

They were back in Lawrence. Despite her dim prospects of graduating, Stacey was still enrolled at KU Law, and she still had to show up there every two weeks to take a class that went along with her internship. Stacey was eating out with Roland again, this time at a cheap lunch eatery near the campus. She told herself it was completely innocent, but then she consciously picked an isolated table in a corner. She sensed that he liked her. She wanted to enjoy that, just for a few minutes, just in that secret corner.

There were good excuses to meet, of course. They were classmates. They were neighbors; his apartment was right above hers. They had gotten to know each other in study sessions for Communications Law class.

"I'm giving up my apartment," she started.

"What? Why?" Stacey noticed he seemed upset.

"I can't afford it. I don't need it. I'm moving back to my mother's house."

"But why there?"

"My brother. My sister. Family problems, I guess you'd say. My internship with Harshaw. It's all in Cosgrove." She shrugged, then watched his eyes. "I'll miss our study sessions."

They both ordered tuna sandwiches and were given their drinks. Reflexively, Stacey started looking for the CTS form on the tabletop. Then she reminded herself that she wasn't in Massachusetts any more. In Massachusetts, it was recommended, though not absolutely required, that all women sign a written *Consent To Sex* form before engaging in intercourse. This had been encouraged as a protection for both parties.

The concept hadn't worked out that well. There had been

some unintended consequences. Bars started handing out blank forms out with their menus, making everyone who wasn't having sex feel like a prude. Some of Stacey's college roommates would sign a whole sheaf of them ahead of time, leaving the space for the boy's name blank. Then they would tape the whole bunch to the outside of their dormitory doors. Some guys started collecting "consummated" forms, comparing them, putting them on the internet. Lawsuits followed about that.

But Stacey hadn't meant to be thinking about sex.

"What?"

"I admire you, Stacey."

A vague sense of excitement was expanding in slow motion inside her chest. But – so soon after Grant abandoned her? And just when she found out she was pregnant? She had learned from her time with Grant that she liked having a man. She didn't have time or energy for a relationship now, not with her world falling apart. Still, she wanted it, wanted him – maybe him. She didn't say anything. Roland looked down, chastened by her lack of response.

"I shouldn't talk like this, I guess," he said. "Maybe Frieda and I got married too young."

"You and Frieda are not happy?" She was shocked at how easily she stepped over the line.

"I love her," – he hesitated for so long the ice cubes in his glass slid down and clicked together – "and part of the reason I love her is her strong moral values. But after two years of marriage I realize I don't share those values entirely. It's not her fault."

"No, I don't think that would be her fault." She stared at him.

"We just ...." He put his hands out, palms up, as if asking for an answer. "We believe different things are important."

"Hm. You disagree with her values." Stacey wasn't going to let him off the hook by talking about *values*. Her pulse raced as she saw his discomfort. She wondered how far he would go. She knew she shouldn't let him. She let him.

"We don't talk any more. She slams her gear in her backpack every morning like she can't wait to get out of my presence." Stacey kept quiet, wondering if he was telling her his marriage was over. "It's my own fault. She's a good wife. I guess I'm such a political animal I want everybody to like me all the time. It hurts a little that the one who knows me best doesn't really like me."

"I'm sure in her heart she loves you."

"If only. But thanks for listening." He gave her a rueful smile. "You're the only person I feel comfortable talking to about this."

"Why?"

"I'm a politician. I have no *real* friends."

"I think you're just feeling sorry for yourself."

She watched him sit back in his chair and accept what she said with a humble nod of his head. "You're right. If I can't look on the bright side of things, who will ever trust me as a leader? But can I tell you one thing I really can't get over?" He kept going before she could stop him. "We hardly ever have sex any more."

"Tell me about it. I know what that's like. Try living 1,400 miles away from your boyfriend for two years."

"But you did it. You're doing it. That's great. You must really love him."

"Actually, it didn't work out. We broke up."

"Oh, I'm sorry."

"Don't be sorry. I mean, I loved him. Or I thought I did. I learned a lot. He taught me a lot. About sex, mostly. I do miss that." She caught his gaze and held it just a little too long.

Chapter 13

Shelbie was acting strange, prancing back and forth outside of Amy's room, whining. Something was wrong. Stacey burst through the door. She had to stop herself from screaming. Amy was wearing only jeans and a bra. She held a razor knife poised just above the skin of her exposed forearm. She had a fresh towel neatly folded underneath like she didn't want to make a mess when she died.

"No, no, no, Amy. You're beautiful, Amy. You're smart. You have friends. I love you. I'm not allowing you to do this." Stacey watched her sister's chest rise and fall and tried to control her own breathing. Mostly she watched the hand holding the knife. She tried not to scream. "Put that blade down, honey."

Amy looked at her sister and raised the knife to her throat. She held her hair out of the way with her other hand. Stacey froze.

"Yeah, like I really have friends. We have to meet in the fields like animals. Every actual real thing we want to do in school is a crime. I can't walk on the street without covering up my mark. I'm sure they'll catch Dad and mark him, too, sooner or later."

"No!"

"It's so horrible, you think. But it already happened to me."

"I'm sorry, Amy." Stacey sat down and, in as natural a motion as she could manage, took the blade from Amy's hand. Amy turned to her, collapsed into her, cried on her shoulder. "You're not really a marko, Amy. You're not an addict, or a convicted felon."

"That doesn't matter." Amy was still sobbing, her tears wetting Stacey's neck. "The vigilantes will do me like they did that man you saw on the street if I show up anywhere. That one with the red beard ...."

"Wait a minute. You know these vigilantes?"

"Not their names. But it's the same guys every time. On motorcycles. There's only three of them."

"Did anybody ever get their plate numbers?'

"Kendrick got close one time to try to read the numbers. They kicked him and said they'd burn out his eyes with acid if he tried it again."

*** ***

"She should file a police report in this office right away." Randy was adamant. "Third degree assault. Kidnapping. Mutilation. If she doesn't report it, the perp gets away with it. Maybe does it again."

"I know," Stacey replied. "But she doesn't want my mother to know about it."

"God, Stacey, people will know." Randy stood up and paced around the office in agitation. His long, bulky frame towered over Stacey. "She's a marko as far as anybody on the street can tell. I hate to say this, but she'll be fair game for other vigilantes, too."

"She knows. She's really depressed. Maybe she could get plastic surgery."

"Illegal in this state to remove a mark. And markos can't travel out. We got to arrest those vigilantes. The state police don't seem to want to help. Governor Adams ordered the KBI to focus on people who are breaking the new religious laws."

"Like Kendrick …?"

"Yeah." Randy was angry. "Big crimes. Like looking up information on the internet for your girlfriend."

*** ***

She had wanted to go. It was a chance to get out of the

house and talk more with Amy. Amy wouldn't let her go with her unless she ditched her phone and laptop, and only if they didn't use the car.

"They're tracking us everywhere, don't you know? Cell phones, laptops, cars."

"Who?"

"I don't know. Conception Control? The KBI? All I know is they always know where you are, and you can't say anything real on any device. Have you already forgotten what's happening to Kendrick?"

After swearing her to secrecy, Amy led her to the garage and showed her the bikes. Amy had her own bike, and she gave Kendrick's to Stacey. After a two- or three-mile ride on narrow roads through the cornfields and a long walk that ended up on dirt path through another cornfield, then over a small hill and under a patch of cottonwood trees, they reached the meeting place.

"This is where my cell meets."

"*Cell?*"

Amy nodded. "We call it that." The skin around her brand was still red. It had just happened the week before. "There's lots of other cells, too. The cops can track every phone, every laptop, every car. So we don't even text. You have to talk to each person you want to come."

"Amy, what I want to know is who did this to you? And why won't you file a complaint with Randy?"

Amy signed at Stacey's naivete. "Randy can't do anything about the vigilantes. They have religious protection. They mark whoever they want."

"This is unbelievable!"

"Believe it. They sell the branding irons online now. Kids can even buy pretend plastic ones."

There was a sudden rustling in the woods behind them. A teenage boy approached them, his shaggy blonde hair catching on the low branches. He was carrying a guitar.

"Tonight?" he said. Amy nodded without introducing him.

"Want some pot?" he asked. Amy nodded again and looked at Stacey.

"What the hell. Me, too."

Maybe it was the pot. Time seemed to stand still, and then suddenly there was a group of about ten or fifteen teenagers under the trees. A girl brought a violin and played little riffs along with the blonde guy playing the guitar. A knot of girls sat in a circle and seemed to be gossiping. Some boys were playing catch out in the field. There was a quarter moon, and bright stars, and no sound but murmuring, and laughter, and the background of the crickets' song. The kids seemed younger, sillier, more carefree than she had pictured them. They could only be this way in secret, Stacey realized.

Amy sat tall, holding her head high so anyone could look at her mark. "It's not so bad," she said to anyone who sympathized. "I always knew I was subhuman. Now it's official."

It seemed like a lot of time had passed, but Stacey couldn't be sure. She checked the path of the moon, and it did seem a little higher in the sky. She and Amy were lying back on a blanket. She didn't expect Amy's question.

"Whatever happened to Foxie?"

"Oh. I guess Dad sold her. When he sold everything else. I remember she was gone by the time I was in college."

"You don't remember exactly?"

"During that time, all I cared about was what I could find to shoot into my veins."

"I always thought, when you went off to college, I'd have riding lessons and all. Like you."

Chapter 14

He drove her to a quiet French restaurant far out in the country. They sat at one of the three tables that were up on a landing a few steps above the main dining room. No one sat at the other two raised tables. Stacey was no gourmet. She usually tried to eat a lot of salads in the hope that she would not grow up to look like her mother, but she was not a foodie by any means. She let Roland order for her, beef bourguignon and Cote du Rhone. She knew she was letting things happen. This wasn't the kind of relationship she had ever thought she would be in. But this wasn't the kind of world she ever thought she'd be in either.

She wondered if he had ever taken a mistress to this secret place. She didn't know for sure if he had ever had a mistress. Was he thinking of Stacey as just that, someone he could fuck on Frieda's fertile days? With a side benefit of tutoring in Communications Law? She had been shaken to the core, wounded badly by Grant's rejection, then flattened by losing her internship at PPD – not to mention the desperate situation of Kendrick in Cosgrove. But she wasn't going to waste any time feeling sorry for herself.

"You let me order for you?" Roland's look was quizzical. "This isn't the hard-charging law student I thought I knew."

"Some men can teach me some things."

He stared off to the side, took a long sip of his wine. She admired his profile. She was glad he didn't respond. She didn't need a cheap, flirty comment right now. Her thoughts went back to Grant, how she had worshipped his calm assurance, his every gesture, his solid male presence. Grant was so stable and balanced she knew it wouldn't take him long to recover from their breakup. His legal assistant Lacee had probably already signed a CTS form for him.

"What are you smiling about?" Roland interrupted her train of thought.

"Oh. Nothing. I was just thinking. Ever since I graduated from college, I got used to thinking I was smarter than most. Better, really – I have to admit. But, you know, real life kind of flattens you out again. You are what you are. What you always were."

This was kind of a test, she realized. Did he know she was talking about her sketchy past history, her beleaguered family, her failed plan to escape it all with Grant?

"Stacey, I don't know what kind of a hole you were in before you came to law school. But I've known you for two years. You've done great for yourself. And now you're reaching back to help your family. You haven't let anything keep you down." He touched her hand.

She pulled it back. Their waiter, cool and efficient, interrupted them. Stacey loved watching Roland fall for her. As much as a politician could fall, anyway.

"You're a delegate. You must be able to do something about what's going on. I mean, my sister was *branded*!"

"Oh shit! I had no idea."

"Women are being burned, raped. And the Certainty Party is somehow getting away with it."

"I swear to you, Stacey, I'm trying. But, see, we Independents are a small minority party. The smallest, after the CP and the Republicans. Smaller than the Democrats, even."

She broke eye contact and slumped in her chair just as the waiter brought her beef bourguignon. She ate a few lumps of the winey-tasting meat.

"I shouldn't take it out on you, Roland. Your party opposed every one of those CP bills."

"So you *do* know what's been going on, politically."

"I researched. I know the Independents almost went along with the CP. I know you're the one who convinced them not to."

"It cost us a lot. We lost some of our big backers."

Now it was her turn to put her hand across the table, touch his arm. "I'm really grateful to you. Every woman in Kansas should be grateful to you."

He met her eyes. "You're the only woman in Kansas whose opinion really matters to me."

*** ***

A few days later, Roland rented a room for them in a small bed and breakfast near the lake. Pregnancy had not tempered her lust, but she was nervous about touching a married man. Roland was obviously thrilled. She caught his excitement as they tore off each other's clothes and fell together onto the bed. His kiss was deep, desperate, but his hands were tentative – something she was not used to. She wanted to be felt, touched, sucked on, used up. She told him what to do. He did as he was told, and then he pushed everything a little harder, a little farther, a little deeper, until she lost all control and cried out so loud the owner called up the stairs to ask if everything was all right. "Everything is *definitely* all right!" Stacey called back from under her new man. They collapsed in laughter. Roland dozed off for a moment, his hand still resting on her cheek. Stacey's body felt limp, spent, totally satisfied, but her mind was racing. What had she gotten herself into? Would he still talk to her now when he woke up?

He did. He said he couldn't talk to Frieda any more. Frieda was CP, he said. She was CP because she had been converted years ago by talk show preacher Reverend Ezekial. Ezekial received the truth directly from God and passed it on to Frieda via *The Prophet* every day. The only thing that kept Frieda and Roland from screaming at each other about politics was Frieda's firm belief that a wife had no right to question her husband's opinion. So she kept silent, and the silence grew between them.

"How did you get involved with her in the first place?"

"We were young and in love. I thought it was admirable that she stuck to her values, even though they seemed strange to me."

"But now? Why are you still married now?"

"She'd never voluntarily give me a divorce. She believes marriage is eternal. Reverend Ezekial preaches that. She believes it. And how could I turn on her when she's actually exactly the same as when we got married."

"And besides, you can get whatever extra you need from me. Right?"

She ran her hand over his body even as she questioned his motives. She used to think Grant was the only one who could get her off, but Roland seemed to be learning fast. Her body had quickened at his touch. But maybe it wasn't the particular man who mattered. Maybe she was the one who excelled at sex.

"Don't make me sound cheap," he protested, his voice resonant as her fingertips crossed his chest. "This didn't happen because Frieda doesn't believe in contraception and there are fifteen days a month when she can't have sex with me. It's much more than that. Like I said, she's a good person. She always looking to do God's will. But she's totally self-contained. She's fulfilled. She doesn't need me at all. I mean, really, she could be married to anybody." He sighed, changed his tone. "I know I'm just a greedy punk who wants a little more than he deserves."

"Like I said, you want to have me on the side."

He took her hand off his chest, held it down to the mattress. "I've admired you for two years, Stacey."

She was shamed out of her sarcasm. "I didn't really mean that. I admire you, too. You're like, my political hero."

"Oh, come on."

"I mean it. You and your Independents are the only people really fighting the CP. Trying to save all the women in Kansas, and all of us, from becoming *subhumans*, really. That's what we would all be. Like markos. Without you and the Independents."

"That's a bit of an exaggeration," he insisted. But he smiled.

"I'll help you in any way I can."

"I need people around me smarter than I am, like you. I'm sure we could fight back together. You make me feel like I could do it."

"Do you love me?" Why not ask? Life was shorter, quicker, tougher than she'd imagined.

"Yes! I'll prove it to you, I promise."

This was so much different from her affair with Grant. So much more complicated. So much more compromised. That's what politicians did, she guessed – compromised. Giving herself totally over to him would be a mistake. He was beautiful, but he was married. He was in love with her, but he would not divorce his wife. All he could do in the legislature was hold his finger in the dike. But at least he was doing that. Stacey thought of Kendrick, of Amy, of the man beaten almost to death on the street. Half the population of the state seemed to be in such a religious frenzy they would burn the other half as witches if Reverend Ezekial told them to. This was the evil Roland was fighting against. She decided she had to drop her pretensions and enter the world of compromise.

"I think I could fall for you," she whispered. She knew this kind of affair didn't usually last too long. But this one had to. And if it was going to be more than just a casual affair, he would need more than normal incentives. She pulled away from him on the mattress. Changed her position. Beckoned to him.

"What are you doing?"

More for him than Frieda would ever do, she hoped.

Chapter 15

Delegate Roland Asher appears to have emerged as the new leader of the Independent caucus. Supporters and critics alike praise his intelligence, his tenacity and his integrity.
– Topeka Capital-Journal

It was 100 miles west of Topeka. It was supposed to be just a hunting lodge, but the place had luxurious rooms on the second floor, each with a beautiful pastoral view through the sliding glass doors which opened onto its own outside balcony. Each room also opened onto a railed inside balcony that over-looked the great room. There was a caretaker, a maid, and a cook. No one else was using the place the night they arrived.

"Roland, how can you possibly afford this place?"

He was getting their suitcases out of the trunk. "It's a long story," he said dismissively – though they both knew Stacey wouldn't take something like that for an answer for long.

"Okay. Explain." They were inside their room now. Roland had told the maid and cook what they needed. Although they obviously knew him by name, he didn't bother to introduce her. She supposed they were used to men bringing their mistresses here occasionally – although the place, with its giant fireplace and rack of dead, horned animals on the walls of the great room, did not seem like a place that would appeal to most women. Stacey guessed mistresses couldn't always be choosy. But she would be more choosy in the future. He had sounded desperate, though, and the idea of hooking up with him again had sent a little thrill of anticipation through her. She reminded herself that he really was a friend and she had always admired him – maybe even lusted after him a little – and she felt entitled to know a little more of his business.

Once in the room, he put his arms around her so fast and kissed her so passionately she couldn't help responding. He was eager and used to calling the shots, but she could make him tentative, make him wait for each move – until she couldn't stand waiting herself. Afterward they lay back in each other's arms and looked out the glass wall of the room as the late summer evening sun painted the landscape a murky, mellow orange. They didn't talk. She raised her head to speak but caught a glimpse of those adoring blue eyes and looked away. She couldn't afford to get lost in anyone's eyes again. Her ear now to his chest, she heard his heartbeat gradually slow.

"I'll show you more," she whispered – and then smiled as she heard his heartbeat quicken. She could do this just by suggestion, but soon the ideas overwhelmed her, too.

This time he fell asleep. She let herself down quietly from the bed and went into the bathroom to clean up. She forced herself not to think about Frieda. She felt she had the right to find out about this guy, to be his confidante as well as his lover. There was no equality. She feared the Professional Reform Act would soon pass, and she'd never be a lawyer. And the situation was much worse the further you got from the capital. In certain counties, the Certainty Party had already began targeting categories of people for subhuman treatment, and there were vicious people on motorcycles who were being allowed to prey on those lower categories: women, addicts, teenagers. She dreaded what else might happen to Kendrick and Amy.

When she came out of the bathroom, he was awake, lounging on the bed, beaming at her in the horizontal sunlight streaming through the glass wall. "I've got a present for you."

"Oh?" Oh, how tacky, she thought. Screw your mistress and give her a bauble.

He got up and rummaged through his backpack. She straightened her clothes and took a breath. Then she was surprised to see him pull out a plain manila envelope and pull a piece of paper from inside and hand it to her. He sat on a chair across the room and asked her to read it. It was a letter of only one sentence.

> *I, Baldwin Touhey, legislative represen-*
> *tative of the forty-second district, hereby*
> *resign from the Certainty Party and the*
> *legislature of Kansas.*

"What! What happened? Did they catch him screwing like, a seven-year-old girl this time?"

"It's my present to you."

"What do you mean?"

"I did that."

"No!"

The explanation was not at all what she had been expecting. In an unusually low voice, he began to tell her a little bit of his life story. "My father died before I was born. My mother worked as an administrative assistant for a company owned by the Golsch brothers. You know, the guys who own half of Kansas and Nebraska and a couple of other states."

"Of course I know them. They're awful."

"Hm. Not to me. They took a liking to me, especially Robert. It's only because of his backing that I've gotten as far as I have."

"So." She sagged down onto the mattress. "That's your function? You're the pretty public face for those oligarch creeps."

He took her hands in his. She felt his tentative gaze before she even turned her eyes up to him. It seemed unfair to her that a man could look this great even when confessing. She felt the tiniest tingling, even then. Was there something wrong with her?

"I've been getting up the nerve to tell you. I was compromised a little right from the start. But I haven't done anything unethical. And I think I can really do some good in the legislature. So far, I'm keeping the Independents from going along with all this crazy CP stuff. But what I want more than anything is for you to be by my side, to help me with that. You're the one who gives me faith I can become my own man politically and, you know, eventually turn this Ezekial mania around."

This kind of adulation made her uncomfortable. "I'm not perfect, Roland. You know I was an addict. I mean, I am an addict. If you know what an addict is, you know I did awful things for a hit."

"Stacey, I don't care what you did as a teenager. I want to be the kind of adult you are. Just give me a chance to try."

She wanted to. She had learned long ago that no one was perfect. And he loved her, she was sure.

"Please, Roland. No more secrets."

"I promise. I swear. No more secrets."

"Come over here. Sit on the bed next to me." He sat next to her at attention like a soldier awaiting orders. "I guess I don't like to be kept in the dark. In politics there's always an explanation, but you haven't been telling me everything. Why don't you tell me exactly what is happening right now? I mean, what do the Golsch brothers have to do with little Baldwin Touhey resigning his seat in the legislature?"

Roland's voice grew stronger as he explained. Apparently, Robert Golsch confided in him almost like a father. He controlled half the newspapers and media outlets in the country. The president had promised Golsch that he could pick the next head of the FCC. Golsch didn't care who the person was, as long as he would follow orders.

"But why in the world would he pick that dolt, Touhey?"

Roland broke into a big smile. "Because I asked him to."

"I'm sorry, but I don't get it. Why did you ask him to appoint Touhey?"

"Because when Touhey takes the FCC appointment, his

seat in the legislature will become vacant."

"So?"

"One less CP vote to override the governor's vetoes."

"Oh. Yeah. I guess that's good."

"And there will have to be a special election to fill his seat. And Stacey Davenport, hometown girl who made good, would be the perfect candidate to go up against the Certainty Party."

Chapter 16

It was a trade. Amy would go to Randy's office and file a criminal complaint against the unknown vigilante who branded her, and in return Stacey would come to the next meeting of Amy's secret circle and tell the story of her addiction.

When Amy and Stacey arrived together at the sheriff's office, Randy immediately settled his large frame in the chair on the other side of the desk in the interview room. Another, much younger guy sat uncomfortably in a small chair to the side, ready to take notes on his device.

"I'm technically family, honey," Randy began, "and of course so's your sister. I know it's a small town and all, but it's still better to have a person who is not related here to witness your statement, so nobody can complain of bias down the road. This here is Deputy Peavey."

Amy barely nodded when Peavey said hello. Randy moved around in his seat uncomfortably. Stacey guessed Randy didn't have much experience dealing with fifteen-year-old girls.

"So, I understand you want to file a complaint about an alleged assault."

Amy rolled her eyes.

"Amy, this is important," Stacey interjected. "There's nothing to be ashamed about. Just tell Randy everything that happened and we can get this over with."

Amy answered Randy's questions, one by one. She brushed her hair aside and let the deputy take a picture of the brand on her forehead.

*** ***

Amy wouldn't call them friends. They were just the people she hung out with sometimes to smoke weed. Sometimes she needed to smoke weed. Sometimes she needed friends who didn't ask anything from her but a little company.

They were in John's Pizza, taking turns running out the side door to smoke, the joint passed hand to hand and always kept outside the restaurant itself. They thought the process was so clever, but John was rolling his eyes. At each of his funny looks, they'd jump up and buy something else. He said he wished all his customers were so hungry. Amy winked at him – not the kind of thing she'd ever done before. He smiled and turned back to the ovens. One of the other girls teased her about it. She didn't care. She felt fine.

Her mother had brushed her off every time she asked about getting her driver's license. She didn't like the feeling of always being a hanger-on, always begging rides, but it didn't bother her that day. She begged a ride home with one of the guys. His motorbike was pathetically small – and so weak it could barely get the two of them up to the 25-mph speed limit. There wasn't much of a seat for her so she put her arms around him and grabbed tight. "Don't get any ideas," she warned him. But it did feel good. He laughed so hard he had to pull over. "Okay, okay, get yourself together. I've got to get home." But the bike was wobbling so much she got off halfway and said she'd walk the rest of the way.

She later guessed she must have been in such a dream state she didn't hear the motorcycle pull up behind her. She remembered having at first only a detached curiosity about her wrists being handcuffed together and manacled to the back of the driver's seat. But as they sped off, an adrenaline shot of fear woke her up. "What are you doing? What are you doing?" she screamed over and over. She didn't get an answer.

The perpetrator was a young guy with a bushy red beard. It was too long a ride. It got dark. He wouldn't take her home. Turned onto a dirt path into a field. Took his helmet off. Tried to kiss her. She turned away. Caught her, knocked her down and chained her on her back between two fenceposts. She thought she'd be raped, but then she heard the hissing of a propane torch. She begged for mercy. No response. Searing pain. Amy was shaking, crying by the end of the story.

"Did he say anything?"

"God told me to mark you."

Amy had to take a break. Deputy Peavey eagerly brought her water and tissues. Then Randy gently but methodically probed her for details. She seemed to feel better as the whole story, with all the details, gradually came out. By the time the interview was finished, the other three people in the room looked at each other. They all had experienced a little of Amy's horror themselves.

Amy left by herself, refusing the Deputy Peavey's offer to drive her home. Stacey asked to stay and talk to Randy. "Not about this." Randy waved off his deputy.

Randy spoke first. "I think it's only two or three guys playing vigilante in this county. I gotta find them before they hook up with Genesis Riders."

"Who are the Genesis Riders?"

"Vigilantes with a cross. Back to the bible people. Way to the back of the bible. Multiple wives, slaves obey your masters, slaughter the infidels."

"Sounds like CP."

"Ezekial supports them. In counties where the Certainty Party is in complete control, the Genesis Riders are given free rein to terrorize anybody they want."

"Aren't the police doing anything to stop them?"

"No, honey, not at all. In fact, over in Neola County, right next door, they're letting the Genesis Riders wear government uniforms – Conception Control uniforms. They have arrest powers. Not on account of any written law. They're just doing it."

She had planned to break the news to Randy that Baldwin

Touhey had quit the CP and the legislature, in the hopes that she could talk him into running in the special election himself. But this new information made her drop that plan. The vigilantes and the Genesis Riders were a much more immediate danger. Who would keep them from taking over Cosgrove County too if Randy went off into politics? Roland was right. She was going to have to be the one to run for office.

*** ***

It was almost midnight, but the plastic cushion on the chair on her mother's porch was still warm from the summer day's heat when she sat down. Kendrick had told her to wait there. She had a moonlit view of the farm across the street and the houses far back from the road on either side. There was no noise but the chirping of crickets. She was wondering why she was waiting there all alone. Then she felt the hand on her shoulder.

"Aaaugh!" The hand closed across her mouth and muffled her scream. She stood up, knocking the chair down, and twisted away just in time to see her father push his ski mask up so she could see his eyes.

"Dad!"

"Hi, beautiful."

Stacey was in shock, but he was laughing, a low comforting sound she hadn't heard in years. He reached out like he still wasn't sure she'd hug him – but early loving memories die hard, and she hugged him tight. It wasn't like she'd ever stopped loving him. It was more like he'd simply been away somewhere all those years when he lived and died for nothing but OxyContin. That OxyContin zombie wasn't her real Dad. Neither was that dull-voiced man she sometimes saw when she visited home from college, that dead-faced creature who spouted platitudes he'd learned in rehab. He laughed now like he was really alive.

"Why are you sneaking around?"

"Can't legally be out at night. Come here."

He was completely clothed in black, and the minute he stepped off the porch he was invisible to her except as a dark blur. She followed that blur around the side of the house. She stumbled on the bike before she saw it.

"Ow!"

"Sorry. My fault. It's pretty much invisible at night. Totally blacked out. No headlight, no taillight. Uses an infrared screen to see. No noise. No tags. Electric. Runs on an old Tesla battery."

"Where did you get it?"

"Made it in my own shop." She should have guessed. "Abandoned machine shop. I make and sell all kinds of stuff. There's a real market for things that actually work."

"Dad, be careful. They're branding people." She didn't have the heart to tell him about Amy.

"I know. Felons and addicts. They haven't got to everybody yet. But branding's not the worst of it. Have you heard about the Make Our Motherhood Strong Act, or MOMS, as they call it?"

Chapter 17

Whump! Whump! I can't do what they tell me.
Whump! Whump! I can't tell what they do me.
– Kendrick Davenport

His phone rang seven times before she hung up without leaving a message. She rang again. And again. And again. She didn't care if it would wake up Frieda. He finally caught on to what she was doing and returned the call.

"I'm in the bathroom." He was whispering. She could hear a faucet running in the background. "Can't this wait until morning?"

"Not if you ever want to see me again."

Yes, he hadn't told her about the Make Our Motherhood Strong Act. Yes, MOMS had enough CP votes to pass. "But it's just another bill that the governor will veto."

"My father says it's the full Ezekial agenda." Stacey's voice was shaking with anger. "Unmarried mothers to be forcibly assigned as second wives with no rights, concubines really, to 'worthy' married men chosen by the clergy. Meaning Reverend Ezekial."

"Yes. And, um, maybe your father didn't mention the sisters. All sisters of any unmarried mother or unmarried pregnant woman are also determined by that law to be morally at risk and in need of a man's control and discipline. Any of them over the age of twelve must be taken away and assigned like the others."

"You didn't think this was worth telling me about?"

"Don't worry. Sweet Fanny Adams will veto that one, too. And it's not going to get a veto-proof supermajority. We Independents are going to hold the line on that one. Hold it a second. Frieda! Business! Get back in bed."

Stacey hung up.

*** ***

She had promised Amy she would talk to her circle about heroin. Her father drove her there on the back of his silent motorcycle. Cars and regular motorcycles couldn't be used to go to these types of secret teenage meetings because their built-in GPS devices, which could not be turned off, would allow the police to track them. Cell phones and laptops were out of the question. Arrangements were made by handwritten note or word of mouth. Kids left their homes with vague excuses. Amy's circle forbade guns, but other groups allowed them. If you drove on the right road at the right time of night, you would pass kids walking with readymade excuses. Asteroid night. Corn maze. Fall adventure. There was an unusual amount of night horseback riding by kids.

When quarterback Cedrick Mohammed in Amy's high school refused to participate in mandatory Jesus prayer and was cut, the whole high school football team quit and challenged the other team to play an unofficial game at night in a field. Fallow Field Football was born. It was so much fun they scheduled other games with other teams. They played on various fields, usually without permission and with very little light. Other groups watched and sometimes joined in. Arguments sometimes arose the next day over who had been ahead when the farmer chased them off.

Kendrick's crew came to the designated place that night. They were only four guys in it. Stacey crept around the edges of the firelight to see what they were doing. She had heard about his rapping in the court hearing, but actually seeing Kendrick doing beatbox almost caused her to faint. She shrunk down to the ground and listened. There were words to his raps too, angry, lonely words, repeated over and over. She wished her mother could see this. She looked back for her father, but he was gone. Kendrick finished and slipped away.

There was a lot of drinking, but it was all fairly quiet. The farmhouse was just out of sight over the top of the slope behind them. She passed some druggies staring at the stars – or at each other, or at something. She hoped this wasn't the group Amy wanted her to talk to. Finally she found Amy sitting by a low fire, alone, and sat down next to her.

"This is really, really nice, Amy."

"It's not always like this. Sometimes there's fights."

"Nothing's perfect. I should know."

"Why did you take heroin?"

She had been planning to meet three or four of Amy's friends, ease into the group, then bare her soul about her drug history. But only Amy had shown up so far.

Stacey began anyway. "Dad left us when I started high school. I felt different, like I couldn't talk to anybody like a normal person any more. I felt this, like, blackness inside. Pressing down on me. It really hurt. It hurt all the time. I couldn't get away from it. Finally, I gave up and decided not to go on living. I kept thinking, hoping really, that killing myself would get rid of the pain."

"I know what you mean."

"Oh, baby. No." She reached out to touch Amy, but her sister leaned away.

"Keep talking," her sister commanded.

"I'm starting the story slow. I'm waiting for your friends to get here."

"I don't have any friends."

Amy's face was lit by only by the flickering fire.

"Okay. I'm not going to give you any you-have-lots-of-friends bullshit like Mom used to give me. The truth is, you can't talk to anybody. The pain keeps pressing you down – and then one day somebody gives you a joint, and you light up, and *oh my God*, all of a sudden the pain is gone."

"I got a question. Why did you feel you deserved to have the pain go away?"

"What?"

"What's different about you, Stacey, is you feel you deserve to be rid of the pain."

"Oh, baby. Have you always been in pain?"

Amy stared into the fire. "Except when I'm working, doing something hard. But talk about you, not me."

"Okay. Well, with drugs, I kind of had friends – other kids who had given up fitting in, too. We'd smoke, cop, inject together. But any of us would steal from any of the others if we needed to get high."

Stacey checked to see if Amy was listening. The story was probably no different than the standard anti-drug lectures they heard in high school. She owed her sister more, no matter what it would cost to tell it. Amy had to know.

"I stole Mom's paycheck. Twice." She definitely had Amy's attention now. Stacey held her sister's eyes. "She blamed it on Dad. I never told her any different."

Chapter 18

We need a warm body that goes to school.
– Don Davenport

She rode back from the clan meeting on the back of her father's motorcycle, sweltering in her black gloves, long black pants, black mask. She leaned into him, her arms around his waist. She couldn't see at all where they were going. The electric motor whined quietly, and so they could talk. She hadn't had a deep conversation with her father in years. But the fog of drugs and rehab seemed to have finally lifted from between them.

"I'd be dead but for you." He was talking about his hideaway room, and the food.

"Grant's money. Amy did all the work."

"I know you started it."

They saw the headlights of a car coming the other way. Stacey's heart jumped as he veered suddenly into its path, then turned away at the last second.

"Are you trying to get us killed!"

"Just a test. Notice he didn't swerve or brake. That means he couldn't see us. That's good."

A test? With his daughter on board? Was her father going nuts? Had he been out there all alone for too long? He acted and talked normally the rest of the way. Stacey decided he was just used to living more dangerously than she was. After they arrived at Audrey's house, he got off the cycle and followed her onto the porch.

"What are you doing, Dad?"

"I'd like to come home."

She could barely see his face in the faint moonlight. She had been ignoring for the past couple of years the evidence that he was his old, cheerful, loving self again. That had made it easier for her to put in the back of her mind how she had compromised him. To this day, her mother thought that he was the one who stole the paychecks the family had so desperately needed. Stacey had now confessed to Amy, but even in this dim moonlight, and even while she was overjoyed to feel his vital presence once again, she couldn't admit this to him now.

"Let's see what Mom says," she ventured. "Let's ask her together."

They didn't have a chance to make a formal proposal. Audrey was standing in the living room fighting down hysterical sobs when they went in.

"Kendrick's gone!"

"No, he's not, Mom. I just saw him rapping at the kids' secret meeting."

She turned and walked away from them, suddenly limping in a frenetic, unstable gait out to the hallway and up the stairs. She came back down carrying something in her hand, sighing with every step.

"His ankle bracelet! He took it off. They can tell! The cops will be after him any minute."

"Um … they won't know." Her father seemed very sure. But he quickly took the bracelet and put it on his own ankle. Stacey and her mother looked at him. "It's actually pretty simple to defeat the electronic lock with a pair of jumper wires and a little software manipulation. But it still needs to sense body heat, so you have to keep the temperature up, too. That's why I couldn't stay out there with Stacey for very long."

"You did this!" Her mother exhaled her panic and replaced it with outrage.

"Yes, I did. The kid wanted to go perform with his crew. Those secret gatherings out in the fields, they're the only place he and his friends feel free."

"You made that decision? You, who don't live here? You, who haven't been here in the last eight years while I raised him?"

Her father's eyes didn't falter. "I'm here now. And I'm planning on being around here a lot. All of our kids will talk to me. I wish you would, too."

Her mother's breathing slowed a little. She gazed across the floor almost like she was looking for something she had lost on the rug – then turned around and wandered out of the room as if in a daze.

"I'll take that as a decent start." The look in her father's eyes was almost merry.

His happiness was contagious. Stacey hadn't felt so optimistic in a long time. Roland might be holding the line in the state legislature, but her father seemed to be doing equally important things. He was showing the kids they didn't have to live in constant fear of Ezekial and his Genesis Riders. And he seemed to be bringing back to her family a spirit of confidence – joy even – that had been missing for so long. She had no doubt her mother would eventually accept him back. His creative, wacky personality was back on display, and she knew her mother couldn't resist that for long.

Kendrick's ankle bracelet was constantly tracked by a computer at the Conception Control headquarters. He was authorized to be only at two places, home and school. Going to school was a condition of his pre-trial release. So he had to go to school, and he did. The twelve hours he had spent in jail hadn't hurt his reputation at school at all. He bonded again with Pete and Jeremy and the one other kid in his crew. The other kids weren't as mean to him as before. He seemed to be doing much better.

That's why Stacey and her whole family were so surprised a week later when he ran away. They didn't even realize Kendrick had split until there was a knock on the door early one Monday morning. It was Corinne. Stacey put a finger to her lips and tried to motion Corinne aside before she said anything that might incriminate Kendrick.

"No. It's not about his case. I just need his ankle bracelet. I said I'd wear it to school for him today."

Corinne claimed she had no idea where Kendrick was. She said he had just left a note for her, telling her the whole KBI would be after him if his ankle bracelet didn't track to school, and asking her to carry it to school and back for him. By the time she finished her story, Stacey's mother and father were on the porch, too.

"Oh my God! Oh my God! If they find out he left, they'll throw him in jail immediately," Audrey cried.

"We can help him, just like this little girl is telling us," her father said, trying to calm his wife down without actually touching her.

Corinne's head jerked up, her shock of bright hair shimmering in irritation at the words "little girl."

"We could all go to jail," Stacey added. "It's a felony to aid a fugitive, and Kendrick is now a fugitive."

"Oh God! Oh God!"

"I'll get the bracelet," her father said as he quickly left the room.

And that's how it was decided. Stacey tried to fit it into Corinne's backpack.

"No. Won't work that way. I'm wearing it."

"The Genesis Riders are doing awful things to any woman who shows any sign of rebellion. I'd hide it under some loose jeans if I were you."

"I'm wearing it."

*** ***

Stacey was out on the porch alone that night talking to Roland on the phone. He was telling her everything now, trying to make up for keeping her in the dark in the past.

"The Professional Reform Act has passed the legislature."

She hadn't yet told Roland she was pregnant. Was this the time to tell him?

Roland ignored her uncharacteristic silence. "It doesn't matter anyway," he went on. "Governor Adams has it on her desk, and she'll veto it."

"And the Independents will stop any attempt to override the veto?"

"That's the plan. If all of the Independents stick together, the governor's veto will stand. All women will still be able to graduate."

Amy came out on the porch just then, and Stacey told Roland she had to hang up. She knew her little sister was disillusioned with her, and she needed to see where their relationship was going now. A three-quarter moon was out in a clear and cloudless sky, and the air was still dry and hot.

Amy didn't mince words. "Dad might not have gone away for so long. I might have had a father, if you hadn't poisoned Mom's mind against him."

"He did most of the other bad things Mom said about him. He stole everything in the house and sold it. He even sold Foxie. He drained their joint bank account."

"But he didn't steal Mom's paycheck."

"What do you want me to say?" She was floating back to that time now. "Back then, I would do almost anything for oxy or heroin. Once it gets a hold of you, Amy, it's hard to stop. I still have to work on resisting it every day."

Amy didn't seem impressed. Or maybe she was just shocked that her whole idea of her family, and her place in it, had been put into question. Stacey found herself desperate to make Amy understand.

"I couldn't stop. I just couldn't stop. But one day my boyfriend, my dealer – same guy – told me to get away from him. Kicked me, actually kicked me away. Like I had caught a disease overnight. I was sad about losing him, but when you're on drugs that's like a little side story. The big story is, where are you going to get your drugs now. Nobody would deal with me."

"So you couldn't get them. So you stopped."

"No. You can't just do that, Amy. I was so sick. I could hardly stand up. But I hitchhiked to Kansas City. Some trucker gave me enough to get a tiny hit on the street, but he called Mom, and Dad came and got me. He forced me into rehab. I tried to kill myself the first night."

"Rehab never works."

"Sometimes it works. Sometimes. I'm proof."

Chapter 19

Now kill all the boys and all the women who have slept with a man. Only the young girls who are virgins may live; you may keep them for yourselves. – Numbers 32:16-18.

"This motorcycle gang, these Genesis Riders, are now branding whoever they want." Randy's face was lined with concern, but his voice was matter-of-fact.

"But – kids?" Stacey was incredulous. "Why would they brand innocent kids like Amy?"

Randy shrugged. "These are the same type of guys I've been dealing with for years. In normal times you see guys like this drunk in bars every night. Half of them smash themselves to death on their motorcycles. And they're always a problem, sooner or later, for any woman they meet."

"But Amy doesn't go to bars."

"They're afraid of women. You combine that with sexual attraction and you get a push and pull that ends up as hate. Then you add Reverend Ezekial saying God wants women disciplined, and you get a bunch of halfwits who decide they have a religious license to take out their hate on any female they run across."

"But why kids?"

"Because they're easy targets. Like markos. You saw what they do to markos."

Stacey swallowed hard. Amy was both a young, attractive female and a marko.

"So why don't you arrest them?"

"There's only three in this county, and we haven't identified them yet. They're not official Genesis Riders – no uniforms or anything. Wannabees, really. But there's forty, maybe fifty real

Genesis Riders in the next county over, Neola."

"There's a sheriff in that county, right? Why doesn't he arrest them? This is assault and battery, torture. These are felonies."

"I'm asking him that question all the time. Him and some other sheriffs."

"And?"

"They're afraid if they crack down on the Riders, Ezekial will say they're soft on sin and the Golsch Brothers will drop their support for them in the elections next year."

"What exactly is the connection between Ezekial and the Genesis Riders?"

"The Genesis Riders are kind of like Ezekial's religious police force. They enforce his religious edicts, mostly the ones about women, and he lets them do whatever else the hell they want." Stacey stared at her uncle, who went on. "You don't think they thought up that biblical name by themselves, do you?"

"This is the scariest thing I ever heard of, Randy." Stacey wondered if she could find a volunteer lawyer to file a lawsuit to stop some of these CP laws from going into effect, but the chances of that working were pretty slim. The U.S. Supreme Court was letting the states do pretty much whatever they wanted. And what good would a court order do anyway, if the sheriffs wouldn't enforce it?

*** ***

She had ignored seventeen of Roland's calls, but when she came back from her meeting with Randy he was waiting for her on her mother's porch.

"What are you here for?" She spat out the words without thinking. "To drag me off to be someone else's concubine?"

"Stacey, I meant everything I said about being inspired by

you."

"I had to find out from my father about the Make Our Motherhood Strong Act! You didn't think I would care? Oh, I guess you were just too busy fucking Frieda."

"Too busy trying to prove my commitment to you. I filed for divorce against Frieda."

"Oh."

"Freida and I just don't believe the same things. Basic things. She is so good, I thought our basic beliefs wouldn't matter. But they do. I need to be with somebody who shares my beliefs, like you."

"How did Frieda react when you told her?'

"*What God has joined together may no man put asunder.*"

"She's going to contest it?"

"Here's her point of view. If we divorce, she can never get married again. Her love life and her chance for family life are over forever at the age of twenty-four."

"I have to sit down."

Stacey asked herself if she really wanted him enough to make him do that to Frieda.

"I've tried to make it up to you, Stacey. Now I've got Robert Golsch to oppose MOMS. That barbaric bill will never get a veto-proof supermajority without Golsch's approval."

"Do you know how much that hurt me, that you were holding back from me all the information about that? I mean, that bill basically turns any unmarried woman who has ever had children into a concubine. Together with their sisters over the age of twelve. To be concubines. Old Testament slaves! Didn't you think I deserved to know that?"

"Of course. It was just ego, I guess. I thought I had it taken care of."

She told him about the Genesis Riders in neighboring Neola County marking people illegally. "They've become like Reverend Ezekial's private militia. And the sheriff there is too afraid of antagonizing Ezekial to stop it."

But Roland looked strangely enthusiastic. "Stacey, there's only one way to fight this. On the ground. Politically. Like I said before. You've got to run for Touhey's seat. You can do it. You've just got to do it, Stacey."

*** ***

A few days later, Randy called her into his office again. "I just got more information from Neola County. The Genesis Riders aren't bothering to brand anybody any more."

"Oh, that's great."

"No, it's not. It's worse. Now they're taking unmarried pregnant women and delivering them to Ezekial. Ezekial decides which married men get to have them as second wives."

"That's the Make Our Motherhood Strong Act. Governor Adams has vetoed MOMS. That is not the law."

"Yet."

"It's not the law!"

"Okay." Randy held his hands up as if she were going to hit him. "You're right. It's not the law. But Sheriff Weakins won't stop it. The Certainty Party approves it. They call it a pilot program in law enforcement-religious cooperation."

Chapter 20

Those who persist in evil shall bear the mark of Cain.
— Reverend James Ekezial

They were at the bed and breakfast at the lake where they had first made love. Stacey noticed that the flowery quilted bedspread and antique furnishings that had seemed so quaint and charming on their first visit were actually a little old and tattered at the edges. The food wasn't quite as good as she remembered it. But the sex was still good. Afterwards, they lay together.

"I left Frieda. You and I can be seen together now."

"Has she filed an answer in court to your divorce complaint?"

"Yeah. She denies all grounds except incompatibility. It takes three years to get a divorce if that's the only ground."

"Three years!"

"Yeah. You know, CP has a bill in, CP-17 or something, that shortens the incompatibility waiting period to 30 days. That's one CP bill I could go for."

"Don't talk to me about CP," she snapped.

His look was quizzical. She realized she'd never talked to him in that tone. Well, it was time they really got to know each other.

"I can be a bitch sometimes." She tried to smile as she said it. She stared into those beautiful blue eyes. The eyes of a man who knew the good and the bad of her and was still in love with her. A man who had made a terrible mistake of rushing into a marriage too young with a religious fanatic who actually had no interest in him at all.

"I want to know the real you, Stacey. If you have a bitchy side, bring it on. I mean it. But I haven't seen anything I don't love yet."

When she had told him she was an addict, he had obviously been shocked. But he had made a point of letting her know that his feelings for her hadn't changed. He knew all about her sordid drug past; now he knew she was sometimes a little bitchy. He knew the secrets of her body – except for one. And he still wanted to get to know her better. He was good in bed. He was fitting in with her plans. He actually was becoming her plan.

Roland was flawed, of course. He'd gotten his start as a political mouthpiece for the Golsch brothers. But everybody was flawed. He was growing into his role as an independent, honest politician. She wanted to help him. And he was madly in love with her. She would marry him now if she could. She could make him forget his sad, sterile years with Frieda. She relaxed now into the crook of his arm.

"I need to tell you a really big secret. A secret that affects the two of us." It was definitely the time to tell him this.

He turned toward her, kissed her, traced her chin, the slope of her nose, ran two fingers down her body, pausing, stroking. He seemed to think there were no secrets between them.

"My breasts aren't always this large."

"What? What does that mean?"

This was the second time she'd made this confession in six weeks.

"I'm pregnant."

* * * * * *

Roland's silence lasted only a minute. During that minute, he looked everywhere but in her eyes.

"I abstained from sex with Frieda two weeks every month just so this wouldn't happen."

Did he think this was all about him?

"You're not happy, are you?" she sighed. She should have known better than to ask. She should have known by now that guys were never happy. She sat up straight on the edge of the bed, wondering if she should just tilt herself forward, get up on her feet and keep going out of the room.

"I'm happy for you." It sounded like he was on the other side of the bed, facing in the opposite direction. "But what a shock! Me, a father? Wow, that's something new."

She had already thought this through. She knew what she had to say. He wasn't stupid. He could count. He would count, eventually. "You're not the father."

He stood up and paced back and forth from the frilly curtained window to the crooked bathroom door held open by the cute little iron statue of a squirrel. "This will be our baby."

"Well, actually …."

"A baby." He stopped and looked out the window, the early morning light emphasizing the paleness of his face. "But it's more complicated than you think. You don't understand …."

"Oh, I understand all right. Actually, I've heard this shit before."

"No." He turned around, a horribly pained look on his face. "You really don't understand. The Professional Reform Act has passed, and now it looks like it is going to get a super-majority to override the governor's veto. Pregnant women will be prohibited from getting graduate degrees. Now you won't be able to graduate."

"You told me you would stop it!"

"I'm still arguing against it, but the Independents are caving to Bob."

"Robert Golsch? What does he care about pregnant women?"

"He doesn't. He cares about the minimum wage. Getting rid of it. He needs the support of the Certainty Party. He made a deal with them."

"Oh Jesus! You're going along with him on both things!"

"No. No." Roland got down on his knees in front of her. He buried his face in her lap. "No, I'm not going along with it. It's caused a lot of friction with Bob – with my mother, even – but I would *never* do that to you. But he's pressuring all the Independents to go along with CP on this one. People are caving."

*** ***

Everyone in her mother's house was feeling the tension. They needed to find Kendrick. Corinne was still picking up the ankle bracelet every morning and bringing it back every day after school. Someone in the house would wear it all night to keep it up to body temperature. The KBI hadn't figured out that he was gone. But Stacey was worried.

"Aren't you afraid you'll be caught?" she said to Corinne one morning. "In fairness, I need to warn you. You could be charged with aiding a fugitive. That's a felony."

"Nothing will happen." Corinne stretched her foot to the top of the porch railing, quite a stretch for somebody her size, and unlatched the ankle bracelet from her impossibly skinny leg with the special escape latch Stacey's father had improvised.

"People are always so sure nothing bad will happen, until it does."

"You don't get it." Corinne's pointy little face seemed to be pointing at her. "Nobody can tell it's real. Ankle bracelets are all the rage. Lots of kids are wearing them to school now."

"What? Where in the world would they get ankle bracelets? You can't buy them legally. You'd have to make them yourself."

Corinne's one foot was still up on the rail. She rolled her eyes and jerked her head toward the house, the movement making her long, uncut hair shimmer. "Your father, of course."

Stacey had been dumped by John Packer and PPD, and her

dreams of using her PPD internship to fight the Certainty Party's laws had been squashed. She had thought she lost everything when she lost those potential allies in Topeka. But she realized now she'd never given Cosgrove a chance. And Cosgrove was coming through. Corinne was tougher than she looked. And smarter. And she knew how to find people who could help. And her father had made good use of that abandoned machine shop.

"You guys are so far ahead of me," she confessed. "And so much braver."

"After we heard about Amy, somebody knocked down a Rider's cycle in town. Now they say they're coming for revenge. Kids are scared as shit."

"Corinne, do you think you can help me find Kendrick? If they find out he's not living in the house, they'll put a fugitive warrant out for him."

"No idea." Corinne drove her hands into her jeans pockets. "He didn't tell me. He could be safe in a blue state by now."

Stacey couldn't believe she hadn't thought of this before. If he got across the border to a blue state, they'd never extradite him, not for Feto-Terrorism, which wasn't a crime anywhere else except in Kansas and a few other red states. The Supreme Court had loosened the rules on extradition as the red and blue states had drifted apart. The United States was really almost two different countries now.

But it was hard to believe skinny little Kendrick had left Kansas entirely. Stacey knew she had to come up with a plan to find him.

** ***

"Why are you against my plan?" Stacey was trying to talk to Amy quietly in her bedroom. She couldn't believe she wasn't cooperating. "It's a chance for me to talk to him in secret, and maybe keep him from getting into even more trouble."

"You have no idea! You've never been branded! Those Genesis Riders are pissed. They threatened on Facebook to brand anybody who's wearing those ankle bracelets."

"I see you're wearing one."

"Of course. I mean, I have to. Dad would kill me if I didn't support Kendrick."

"What I'm asking, Amy, takes a lot less courage than what you've already done. Just see if you can get up another meeting, you know, out in the fields – what do you call them, *circles*? – and include Kendrick's rapper friends again. He'll find out. He won't be able to resist coming to perform. But then I can talk to him there as his lawyer. And he won't have to tell me where he's living."

"I'm saying, you just don't know these people, how vicious they are."

"I'm saying, you can do this. For your brother. Corinne already said she would help."

Chapter 21

In addition to her own questionable moral background, sources tell us that Miss Davenport has close family members who are markos and terrorists. – WKTK Action News, Cosgrove, Kansas.

Amy's circle overlapped somewhat with Kendrick's rapper crew, who overlapped with the Fallow Field Football gang, who overlapped with other groups. Gatherings happened suddenly, with little notice, and they dispersed just as quickly if the police or the school authorities found out. There was a huge increase in vandalism at the schools. Some of the kids were carrying guns to school. The idea had spread that sooner or later Conception Control or the Genesis Riders were coming after them and they had better be prepared. Some of the kids seemed ready to fight back. One night someone shot up the Certainty Party's headquarters in Topeka.

There was some risk in holding a meeting two weeks after the last one. The farmer whose field had been trespassed on last time had discovered beer cans and the remains of several bonfires and had called the police. The farmer was quoted later in the *Cosgrove Cosmopolitan* as regretting that he had ever reported it, as an army of state police, SWAT teams and forensic investigators overran that part of his farm for a good part of a week – testing, they said, for evidence of terrorism. "They did a hundred times more damage than those kids ever did," the farmer was quoted on the news.

Randy's sheriff's department did not participate. "We're spending all our resources right now looking for the men who beat a man almost to death, putting him in the hospital, where he's still in critical condition. We've got other serious assault cases unsolved. The only allegation I've heard so far is kids partying in the fields. Let the KBI investigate that all they want."

Corinne helped Amy organize the next meeting. She delivered the coded message to every person in the school wearing an ankle bracelet. The special instructions were that this gathering would have a musical performance theme. Amy worked the high school strictly by word of mouth. Stacey's father located a spot, just out of sight of the road bordering the far side of the Westerfield farm. But no one, not even Corinne and Amy, would know the exact location until the afternoon of the event. Kendrick's friends Pete and Jeremy spread the word that they were absolutely performing, and that Kendrick would be there. Neither of them had actually talked to him, but they were pretty confident he wouldn't miss it.

Stacey could sense a groundswell of disgust among all the students at the constant surveillance of all their electronic devices. Nothing else could explain the completely impractical, probably illegal but wildly popular secret events. These kids had no real power – or even any understanding of how to change things. And none of them could vote. She knew her parents were outraged at the Certainty Party and the Genesis Riders, but most of the other adults in Cosgrove didn't seem to care, or else they were afraid to talk. Some adult, somewhere, needed to have the nerve to tell people what was going on and give them courage to speak. They needed a knowledgeable and articulate adult. Stacey really hoped it didn't have to be her.

Stacey called to make an appointment to see Randy in his office. "How dangerous would it be, really, for me to run for state delegate, for the seat Baldwin Touhey just vacated?"

"Definitely somewhat dangerous."

"I mean, specifically, what are the dangers."

"Okay. Those Genesis Riders are dangerous people, but there's not many in this county. As long as you stick to Cosgrove and stay out of Neola, I can protect you."

"Is it that bad in Neola County, really?"

"The sheriff in Neola County has turned them completely loose. They're rounding up unmarried women. They started to auction them off online, but Sheriff Weakins at least had the guts to stop that."

"So he stopped them?"

"No. He stopped them from auctioning them off. Now they're selling them to Reverend Ezekial to be assigned."

*** ***

Roland was ecstatic she was running. He drove to Cosgrove every chance he got, even though she wouldn't let him sleep with her in her mother's house. "I'm a total, complete novice to politics," she told him as they sneaked an embrace one evening on her mother's front porch. "I mean, I don't even know step one."

"I'm a total novice at being a father. So maybe we're even."

He said she needed an office, and signs, and an organizer in each precinct, and a media budget. He estimated she needed $40,000 just to get started.

She was shocked at the amount. "There's no magic way that my candidacy might just catch on?"

"You need 40K just to get people to recognize your name."

She knew where he was planning on getting this. Forty thousand was just the tiniest crumb to Roland's mentor, Robert Golsch.

"What would I have to do?" she asked. "Promise to vote to abolish the minimum wage? Promise to allow him to take over *all* media in Kansas?"

"It's not that cut and dried. I'll tell him you're a good person. He'll take my word for it. He might ask you for some favors down the line. You make your decision then. If you cross him badly, you can expect your opponent in the next election to get at least 250K funding from him. And, of course, he'll be pissed at both you and me."

"I'll take my chances if you will. Get me the money."

He got the money, and she opened an office and paid for an ad in the Cosgrove newspaper and started searching out and talking to people her mother knew and those few acquaintances she remembered from high school. She needed at least one organizer in each precinct. Her father traveled illegally to the office at night and pulled the shades down, and he produced a list of new names for her to contact every morning. She put two giant American flags in the front window of the office, and that seemed to be working to keep the Genesis Riders at bay, at least during the day. Her father told he would provide the nighttime security. She didn't know what he meant, and she didn't want to know.

It didn't take long for her CP opponent, Bradford Bullins, to point out that her brother was an indicted terrorist. He even invented a nickname for her, "Sister Terror," and it was repeated ad nauseam in the trending media and even on television news from Topeka – until Robert Golsch ordered it stopped. But this focus on Kendrick's indictment made it all the more important for her to find Kendrick and bring him home before he was caught.

Chapter 22

All student papers will be screened for crude, vulgar or obscene material, or any material that questions the Divine authorship of the Holy Bible or the truth of any of its teachings. Any student whose paper violates this rule will be immediately suspended. – Cosgrove High School Student Handbook.

The dried corn was eight feet tall, blocking the view from the road. Past the gently clacking cornstalks, over a little rise, behind a tiny stand of trees beside a pond, the secret meeting was growing. Twice, Stacey had crammed four kids and their bikes into her mother's pickup and dropped them off a mile from the site. When she arrived herself, a lot of the kids were drinking, and she could smell the sweet odor of pot in the air. There was just enough light that she could see that some of the kids were wearing their fake ankle bracelets. Corinne had left her genuine ankle bracelet at Stacey's mother's house. They'd found a way to put it around Shelbie for body warmth. Stacey found Corinne by the glow of her silvery hair.

"Is Kendrick here?"

"Dunno. Kids here are spread out, doing their thing."

"He could be anywhere. I'll never find him."

"Find him by ear, of course," Corinne acted surprised Stacey was so clueless. "When you hear him rapping."

Stacey couldn't find Amy at first. She'd assumed her sister would be alone like the last time, but now she found her huddling near a bush on the edge of the pond with three or four other high school kids, smoking pot. She crept close, not wanting to show herself and possibly mess up Amy's new friendships. They had a tiny little fire going which they were using for light as they doled out the pot. The moon was so bright they hardly needed it. And they all seemed to have flashlights anyway. Stacey caught Amy's eye and noticed that she had her hair pulled back in a ponytail and wasn't trying to hide the mark on her forehead. A sudden flashlight beam now focused on that mark. Amy flinched for just a second, but then she stopped and explained to the group how she got marked. She shrugged, raised her eyebrows, gestured with her hands – all with a sour smile on her face. But at least it was a smile.

There weren't enough players for Fallow Field Football, but some of the boys was played anyway, three against two, with the third player changing sides after each score. The game was going on in the field right next to the pond, orange reflective wristbands versus green reflective wristbands, the football a kind of fluorescent blue. Stacey stumbled onto other kids gossiping, reciting awful poems, making out – and finally, two hundred yards from the pond, at the top of a small rise, facing back toward the rest of the kids as if they were imagining they were playing in an amphitheater, the musicians.

She trudged cautiously through the little dip in the field between the pond and the higher ground where the musicians were playing, carefully stepping around any kids lounging on the ground. There were more celebrants here than back at the pond. Someone was playing an ironic folk song on a guitar. Kendrick and his friends were not in sight. But she didn't think he would pass up this chance to perform.

She stepped around a couple avidly fondling each other on a blanket. Then she heard a voice call Jeremy's name. Jeremy was Kendrick's friend, and the cause of Corinne's pregnancy – if Corinne had ever been pregnant. Stacey felt a sting of resentment that Jeremy had been let totally off the hook while Kendrick now faced twenty years to life in jail. If Jeremy was here, Kendrick would be here, too. But she couldn't hear Jeremy's answer now because a folk singer in the group suddenly found his voice.

Don't need no fuckin aaaan-kle bracelet.
We'll tell you where we traaaack.
Back to the fields where freedom is real
And we're never coming baaaaack.

A few big kids standing shoulder to shoulder blocked her vision. Stacey's heart jumped when she thought she caught a glimpse of Kendrick's face behind the singer, but then he disappeared. The song seemed to be over, and the huge boys started to move out of her way – but then there was some more loud strumming, and everyone grudgingly stopped.

Oh, nothin rhymes with aaaan-kle bracelet ...

Okay. She was glad nothing rhymed with ankle bracelet. People were moving on, finally.

Oh, nothin' rhymes with aaaan-kle bracelet
You can see the fix I'm in.
I'm out here down with the pigs and the possums
Committin' the original sin.

The singer kept strumming, but he couldn't think of words fast enough to keep their attention. The two big kids pushed up against him, and someone gently took his guitar and handed it to his friend. Just then she saw Kendrick. She got close enough to grab his shirt before he even noticed her.

"Kendrick, you've got to come home."

He shrugged out of her grip. "Everybody hates me there." He turned away. "I'm on next."

She followed him and grabbed him by the wrist. "Listen. I think I can get you off. But you're making yourself into a federal fugitive. That's a crime in itself – even if you aren't guilty of Feto-Terrorism. You could go to jail just for fleeing."

He pulled his wrist free and mumbled something.

"What?"

"Let's see how this goes."

He walked away toward the top of the rise where Jeremy and Pete were waiting. He seemed more worried about how he was received by the kids in the audience than in his status as a fugitive. There wasn't much of an audience, maybe ten or fifteen kids standing around. Stacey noticed the flare of Corinne's hair near the back of the crowd. Of course! She should have recruited Corinne to talk to him. Maybe it wasn't too late. She had just started working her way towards Corinne when the whole event was suddenly stopped short.

A roar of engines ripped through the air, and the bright headlights of motorcycles crashed out of the corn. Instantly, everybody was running, crawling, rolling out of their path. The motorcyclists roared down one edge of the dip almost to the pond, then came back up the other side. They circled around, their exhaust fumes mixing with the clouds of dust in their headlights while the crowd of teenagers panicked. Stacey screamed for everyone to put their flashlights on. She wanted to see if one of them had a red beard. The lights shining in their eyes bothered the riders, so they aimed their motorcycles at whoever was trying to blind them.

The kids shrank back up the hill where the motorcycles couldn't follow, and eventually most people were out of their reach. Still, they circled. Then they stopped. Stacey kept shining her flashlight until she saw a red beard. That motorcycle turned to aim directly toward her. She turned off her light and dove to the side, but that motorcycle turned away before it was even close to her. She pushed herself to her feet. A few teenagers, half of them drunk, were venturing into the circle and taunting the riders, shining lights right in their eyes. Corinne was one of them. All three riders stopped and looked toward each other as their engines idled.

"Run! Get away now!" Stacey yelled to Corinne and the other teenagers, but they couldn't hear her. Nobody could hear what the riders were yelling at each other. Suddenly, the one with the red beard turned and blasted his way out through the corn. That seemed to anger the other two riders. One reached into the other's saddlebags. Stacey held her breath, waiting for him to pull out a gun.

Instead, the rider brought out a chain. Stacey flashed back to the scene she had witnessed on Greyson Street. These were those same two guys who beat that poor marko almost to death. The local Genesis Riders. But before Stacey could think, the lead Rider was swinging the chain in a wide circle and advancing toward the kids. The kids ran, but they were not all fast enough. Stacey could clearly see in the motorcycle headlights a tall, skinny boy who was about to be hit. Running frantically, he tripped and fell flat on his face just as the chain whizzed overhead. The Rider with the chain screamed in outrage and kept going. The other Rider followed and ran over the kid's leg with his motorcycle. The kid got up, and two friends helped him limp away.

They were chasing Corinne next, and she wasn't going to make it. Stacey screamed desperately for her to hit the ground. But as the Rider with the chain rose up to whip her, he was suddenly thrown backwards off his motorcycle and flat on his back. The empty cycle scraped by Corinne and fell, still rumbling, and started a small fire in the dry grass. Corinne stumbled, fell down, then sat up. The second Rider rode cautiously down toward his companion, but his fear was obvious. Some of the kids had regrouped on the side of the hill and were throwing rocks at him. Suddenly at a disadvantage, this last Rider revved his cycle and crashed away through the corn.

One kid yelled he knew how to turn the motorcycle off, and

others started to stamp out the fire that was creeping toward the fallen Rider. He didn't move. Gradually the teenagers pulled away, then turned and ran out of the field. Stacey had not heard a shot. She came close and shined her flashlight on the Rider. He was a young guy with dark hair, a round, sweaty, really pale face. She didn't recognize him.

His helmet began filling with blood as she stared. She gagged, then forced herself to try to take it off. She yelled for Corinne to help, but there was no answer. Stacey finally got the helmet off. The Rider coughed up blood for a long time. Then he went totally limp, his open eyes staring blankly. His gurgling attempts at breathing stopped. His skin was blue in the light from her flashlight. She was sure he was dead. Stacey couldn't stop herself from shaking. Her knees buckled and she collapsed to the ground.

She made herself get up. No one else was left in the field. As her flashlight beam trembled over the ground, she found exactly what she was afraid to find. She froze for a moment, then took a deep breath, reached down, and picked up the murder weapon. Then she wiped her fingerprints off his helmet and walked away.

Chapter 23

Terrianne will be there to meet and greet you all, and maybe give you some tips on looking your best. – Advertisement in the *Cosgrove Cosmopolitan*.

Stacey knew she must be entering a strange new world when she found herself asking her mother for advice. When she explained that there was a good chance the Professional Reform Act would go into effect, her mother started to unravel completely, whining like a wounded dog. "I knew they would take away everything from me, but I thought you, at least you, would escape."

"Mom, get a grip. We have a chance to fight back, right here in Cosgrove. All the kids are already against CP."

"Nobody cares about the kids. They don't vote. Oh, honey …."

"Please, Mom, no more *oh honeys*."

"Oh, honey. Oh, sorry. Ahem. Stacey, I'm so scared for you. They're taking women away right in the next county over, Neola County."

"So, do you get it, Mom? I want to stop that stuff from happening here. Somebody's got to speak out against this. You know I signed up to run for Baldwin Touhey's seat."

"I'm so scared."

"Mom, for just a minute, can you forget about being scared and help me instead. I need to talk to people, tell them there's hope. That's where I need your help – to talk to the women. While they still have the vote. I don't really know anybody in Cosgrove County any more."

"You know, when I was young, I planned on being smart like you. I gave up everything to marry your Dad."

Stacey had heard this story a hundred times before. At least her mother now skipped the last part, the part where her addict husband turned into nothing but a drugged-out specter who left her broke and heartbroken. Her mother had no idea how much guilt Stacey felt each time she was forced to listen to this story.

"Mom, be smart for me now. You know everybody in this town. Especially the women. You're out there talking to them all the time. Isn't there some way you can help me meet them? I have some money."

*** ***

The Cosgrove Fall Fashion Show was a big hit. They brought in Terryanne, a famous model from New York who was rumored to be one of Robert Golsch's girlfriends. The first time she walked out on the homemade runway, which Stacey's father had built, a friend of Audrey's felt the need to comment in a loud voice.

"That's a *dress*? I couldn't even get one of my legs into that thing."

Audrey had arranged for a few high school girls to model similar skinny dresses. The women were very sweet to the girls, but a lot of them were wondering out loud who would actually wear dresses like that. Audrey and Stacey were passing around white wine. The snide comments about the dresses got louder as the wine flowed.

"And now," Stacey suddenly announced, "we're going to show some of the latest children's styles."

A line of more than half the class of Cosgrove High solemnly gathered behind the runway. The boys walked first. There was nothing special about their clothes, but each one was wearing an ankle bracelet as they walked in with a strange, slow goose step. Then they stopped, raised their braceleted legs like warnings, and spun slowly around in the air. There were a few giggles and lewd comments from the crowd at first, but the commentary faded when the boys didn't crack a smile. The demonstration went on long past the time the novelty wore off. The crowd was still hushed when the boys finally filed off the runway and goose-stepped through the crowd toward the exits without making eye contact with anyone.

Then the girls slowly walked the same path. Their clothes were ordinary and varied and without any discernable pattern, but the unifying theme was the brand that each one had stamped on her forehead. They paired off, then bowed to each other until their foreheads touched. They held that position in silence until everyone in the room was uncomfortable. Then slowly, eyes to the ground as if they were truly in bondage, they marched to the exits.

Stacey stood on the runway alone with a microphone.

"I'd like to talk to you all seriously for a moment about what is happening in this state."

Her knees were shaking. This wasn't like giving your smart-ass opinion in a law school class. Half the women here remembered her reputation as a bad influence, an addict, a girl who got away from it all even as some of their own children succumbed. Roland had come up with various ways to treat her history, make her past into a talking point, a success story people could look to as a model. Stacey decided to ditch all that. She hadn't yet even come to terms herself with all that she had done. When it came down to it, it didn't really matter who she was. She had to tell people what was happening to *them*.

"Half the children in the middle school and high school are wearing mock ankle bracelets. They're doing this in solidarity with my fourteen-year-old brother Kendrick, who could spend twenty years in prison for looking up something on the internet." Stacey decided she didn't need to go into detail. Half of these women had boys. They knew what crazy shit could happen with boys.

"You saw the girls walk the runway here, pretending to be branded, humbled. My sister was kidnapped and branded for real by the Genesis Riders. The Genesis Riders are a violent motorcycle gang pretending to enforce the Certainty Party's new laws. A lot of us saw them brutally beat a man right on Greyson street a few weeks ago.

"In Neola County, right next door to us, the Genesis Riders are rounding up unmarried pregnant women and giving them to Reverend Ezekial, who assigns them as second or third wives to married men. As concubines. They have no rights, not even the right to keep their own children.

"But the worst thing is, it will all be perfectly legal if the Certainty Party's new bill, the Make Our Motherhood Strong Act, becomes law. Make Our Motherhood Strong. They call it the MOMS Act. Sounds nice, doesn't it? I call it the Right to Rape Act. If that bill becomes law, no woman will be safe.

"I'm running for the Kansas House of Representatives to stop MOMS from becoming law. I know I'm not the perfect candidate. Many of you may have memories of me from when I was a teenager, from a time I'm not proud of. But this is not about me. This is about you. We all should be fighting the Certainty Party. Your future as free women is at stake.

"So please think about it. Please vote for me. Your own rights are at stake. If we don't all act together now, this may be your last chance to vote at all."

Chapter 24

She felt sweaty and weak by the time she arrived for their rendezvous at the bed and breakfast. She collapsed into Roland's arms.

"Running for office is so much harder than I thought. Hold me. Tell me there's an end to the endless meetings, the endless false attacks on me by the CP."

"Politics is as tough as people think." He pulled back to see her face. Smiled. "But you're doing great. We had a poll taken, and you're at 28% name recognition. That's phenomenal for someone who was an unknown a few weeks ago."

"Some of the women are catching on. The men? Honestly, I think a lot of them would like to have an extra wife or two."

"Not this man. You know that." His smile was beautiful. "All I want is to be with just you, all the time. And of course, one day, with our child."

She broke eye contact, walked toward the bed and sat down. "I wish we could be together more."

He sat down next to her. "I miss you when you're not here. Everything I've ever wanted to do, in any aspect of my life – it seems possible when you're around."

"How's Frieda?"

He shrunk back. "Why do you say that? You know I filed for divorce."

"I was thinking about the CP, and the idea of multiple wives. You actually do have one and a half wives already."

"You're blaming me for that? Years ago I married a serious woman who later became a religious fanatic. Now, because of that, she won't let me go without a legal fight. So shoot me." He stood up testily, paced the room. He picked up something from the bureau with trembling hands and stared at it. "This came in the mail to your old apartment. It didn't fit in the mail slot. Frieda picked it up."

It was a postcard from Grant. *You told me not to email you. Saw that you're running for Kansas legislature. Congratulations. You would be perfect!*

"What? Are you jealous?" She raised an eyebrow.

He took both of her hands in his. "Yes. It bothers me. Why are you getting postcards from him?"

"I don't know." She jumped up. "Maybe because I told him never to call me, text me, email me, snapchat me or tweet me." Her little edge of anger faded. Of course, Roland was upset. She was sorry she snapped at him. They found themselves together on the bed again. Afterwards, they both fell asleep. She woke first, sat up and checked her phone.

"Oh my God!" She shook his shoulder violently. "It happened, like you predicted. The legislature overrode Governor Adams' veto of the Professional Reform Act. It's the law now. So much for me getting my law degree."

"Stacey, you've got to believe me. I fought that bill so hard Bob Golsch isn't even speaking to me."

"You *knew* the veto was overridden, and you didn't tell me?"

"I was going to tell you, after …."

"… after you had me one last time?"

"No. No, that's not true. I fought against it with everything I had. I know how hard you've been working to get your degree. You'll have all your credits by the time you finish your internship. You've got to keep going. Don't give up now. We'll get this reversed somehow." This spirited, fighting Roland was the Roland she loved best. "We've got to organize now, like you said, threaten the school that *all* the women will withdraw if the school obeys this law."

He collapsed on his back, staring at the ceiling covered with its silver fleur-de-lis imprints. Stacey was trying to re-orient herself to her new status as a person who could never become a lawyer or get any type of graduate degree. The Certainty Party's plan to subjugate women seemed to be succeeding, step by step.

"The CP is calling a press conference to announce how they want the law implemented," Roland said, still staring at the ceiling. "Why don't we watch it. Maybe they'll grant an exception to women who are already in school."

But nobody from the Certainty Party spoke on the screen. Instead, Reverend Ezekial stood behind a pulpit. "This is a great victory, God's victory over the modernists, the liberals and the secularists who have ignored or ridiculed the teachings of the Holy Bible." On the screen, Ezekial looked as if he had been packed into his dark suit like a sausage. His hair was too bizarre for the self-satisfied look on his face. The look faded quickly anyway. Ezekial said he was not satisfied with just passing the Professional Reform Act.

"We are not finished by any means. God has made clear that women are the *weaker vessel, 1 Peter: 3:7*, but necessary for purposes of breeding. What does the Holy Bible tell us about the importance of breeding? *When Leah saw that she had stopped having children, she took her maidservant Zilpah and gave her to Jacob as a wife. Genesis 30:9*. His other wife, Rachel, did the same. Over and over again, God has revealed to us that women are prone to sin and immorality and thus in grave moral danger without the loving but strict discipline by a God-fearing man. *Wives, submit to your husbands. Colossians 3: 117-24*. Moses and Jacob and Solomon and David, not to mention Mohammed and Joseph Smith, all had multiple wives. These multiple marriages are God's way of bestowing the blessings of guardianship and discipline that all women need. Especially fallen women. And so I promise to you we will make this compulsory in all of Kansas.

"The Professional Reform Act is thus only step one. God has blessed us with this great victory, but we have even bigger victories to come. God willing, the Make Our Motherhood Strong Act, or MOMS as I like to call it, will be enacted into law before this legislative session is over. Women who have lost their virtue will be gathered by the Lord God Our Shepherd and taught to live a saintly life. We will walk in the footsteps of Jacob and Rachel and Leah and Zilpah.

"I'm putting my hand on the Holy Bible here, and I can feel the power of the Lord welling up in my soul. I feel the power! I feel the power! I feel the power! I know I am His instrument. His power is indestructible, it can't be stopped. It can't be stopped. And so help me God, MOMS will become law, and all of Kansas will learn to live by the words of the Holy Bible before the end of this year!"

Stacey turned to Roland, dejected. "He's never going to be satisfied until every woman in Kansas is a slave." But this wasn't really a surprise. She was wondering more right now about her own life plans, and about Roland. "Why didn't you tell me before that the veto was overridden and the Professional Reform Act is now law? That I can never become a lawyer now." She wanted him to see she was taking this personally.

"I couldn't bear to tell you the whole story. I fought against it hard, so hard Golsch now says I betrayed him. He hates me now. He's cut off all funding for my political action committees. Yours, too. We're both on our own, politically."

"Oh."

Roland switched the TV off. He turned to her, started to say something, stopped.

"What?" Stacey sensed this was something worse.

"This other part, it's kind of just a personal problem."

"*Just* a personal problem? Come on, Roland. Tell me."

"It's my mother. I can't believe this is happening. My mother has turned against me. She says I'm a complete ingrate. She says I stabbed my father in the back."

"Your *father*?"

"I didn't mean to say that."

"Robert Golsch is your *father*?"

He started to cry. She felt the tenseness in the muscles of his arms. She asked him again, demanded really, that he answer.

"I actually, really, don't know. I guess I've always been afraid to find out. But somehow, she – my mother I mean – she acts like he's some kind of god, like all she wants in life is for me to be like him." He turned to her, all the certainty drained out of his face now. Only those blue eyes held it together. "I envy you so much. You have a family. You're *planted* in Cosgrove. I never really belonged anywhere. Maybe that's why I went into politics. When you're a legislator, everybody wants you – or at least wants something from you."

"I believe in you. You're good at it."

"It's such a façade. I was just playing a part. I really wish I could be more like you – you know, a real human being, with a real family, planted in the earth."

Chapter 25

Reverend Ezekial invited her to lunch. He said he wanted to meet the young woman who had the nerve to oppose a CP candidate. His church had the biggest congregation of any church in Neola County, and his TV and internet ministries were million-dollar businesses. The church itself was a large complex of clean brick buildings set far back from the road.

His office was sunny and inviting, with low, wide windows on three sides and bright yellow leather chairs. In person, Ezekial looked a little older than he did onscreen. His fully-packed suit, round face, dark comb over and horn-rimmed glasses looked the same. Stacey couldn't believe he had persuaded millions of people that he was the personal messenger of God. He looked more like an accountant who hadn't made it to the top of his trade because he spent too much time at lunch with his clients.

Ezekial had obviously never been handsome, but he had penetrating grey eyes and an intimidating air of self-assurance. Ezekial actually did own an accounting business, as well as the biggest catering business in the county, and the first phase of his multi-million-dollar Bible Land housing complex was already under construction.

Stacey knew that Ezekial never went anywhere without his personal assistant, Bradbury. Bradbury was the physical opposite of Ezekial: tall, well-built, muscular, shaved head, immaculately dressed, and so silent as to be scary. He sat in the corner of the room during the conversation, immobile except for his eyes.

"Do you realize what is happening as a result of your preaching?" Stacey started. "Women in Neola County are being kidnapped, raped, and given as property to strange men."

Ezekial swiveled comfortably in his chair, swiveled back to

focus on Stacey's eyes. His expression grew cold. "Men chosen by the clergy."

Stacey's jaw dropped. "To be made into concubines – their children his property also, to be used however he chooses."

"David had 300 concubines. *Deuteronomy 17: 16-17.*"

Stacey sighed. This man was lost somewhere in the most barbaric verses of the Old Testament. He wanted to go back to those times. He was clearly imagining himself with a harem, while Stacey doubted that, back then, he would have qualified for even one wife. Not if looks had anything to do with it.

"Oh. Okay. So you really are in favor of this." Stacey stood up. "I guess I don't have anything more to say to you. Thank you for your time." Stacey stared for a second at the stoic statue of Bradbury, then started to go. But then she turned back. She could feel Ezekial still looking at her.

"Reverend Ezekial, satisfy my curiosity. If this becomes the actual law of Kansas, will you personally take women offered to you as concubines?"

"It's all in accord with the Bible."

"That's not my question."

"Yes. Yes, I will." His smile was to himself, not her. "I'm looking forward to Kansas's law changing, coming into conformity with God's law."

Stacey took a breath. "Okay. Good to know." She started to turn again to go, but he wasn't finished.

"As an emissary of God, I look forward to having my choice of which unfortunate, corrupted women to take under my wing and discipline according to God's will."

"Thank you." She turned to go again.

"I've put a lot of thought into this. You might want to hear my plans," he called after her. She turned back yet again. "I can tell you I would choose at least one healthy, intelligent, competent young woman. Someone who could help me manage my businesses during the day, function as my household servant in her free time in the evenings – and of course perform other duties as required at night."

Ezekial smiled again. "Someone like you."

*** ***

Roland's eyes lit up. "Here's something I can do! I've talked to the university's legal clinic. They're already drawing up papers for a lawsuit."

"Come on, Roland. Like the University is going to let its law school's legal clinic sue it? Or sue the state? To overturn the Professional Reform Act that was just passed by a two-thirds majority of both houses of the Kansas legislature? No way."

"No. Not that law. Not any law. The Genesis Riders are abducting women and girls in Neola county right now."

"I know. And Sheriff Weakins there is letting it happen."

"These are crimes, kidnapping, rape, false imprisonment, even in Neola County. Several people have filed affidavits saying that Ned Weakins, the sheriff of Neola County, has told them he has no intention of charging the Genesis Riders with any of these crimes as long as Reverend Ezekial approves of the way they're doing it. So now the law clinic is suing the sheriff, asking that the federal court enjoin him to enforce the laws against kidnapping, rape and false imprisonment."

"Oh, that's great!"

"Yeah, it's good that they're trying. But the abductions are done at night, pretty much in secret. The parents and relatives are terrorized and too afraid to complain. As far as the legal paperwork goes, the case is ready to go. But we don't have any actual proof. We don't have a live plaintiff."

"Women from Neola are pouring into the shelter in the Cosgrove Baptist Church. They're trying to get away from the Neola Genesis Riders. I'm sure one of them will sign on."

"Not good enough. We need an affidavit from a live plaintiff.

Somebody who this actually happened to. I don't think you have anybody like that in that shelter. Is there any way you can find someone who's actually been kidnapped?"

Chapter 26

If you see a comely woman among the captives and become enamored of her, you may take her as your wife. – Deuteronomy 21: 11

Clouds obscured the moon. Only the infrared camera could make out the road's dark tunnel through the tall, drying corn. The black motorcycle with its two black-hooded riders was invisible even to oncoming traffic. The round trip to Neola City, deep into Neola County, would stretch the limits of even the Tesla battery. There had been no lack of volunteers, but Stacey had insisted on being the one.

"I don't understand." Talking was fairly easy with only the sound of the wind to overcome. She put her lips almost to her father's ear. "What they're doing is illegal. So, the Genesis Riders wouldn't keep records of what they did. The county wouldn't keep records either. So how do we find the women?"

"Think about it."

"You know where to go?"

"Already been there."

There was plenty of time to think and nothing to look at, so she thought about it. But her mind wandered. So much had happened. Audrey wasn't much of a churchgoing woman, but she had a lot of friends who were. Buses of pregnant women, unmarried women with children, and their sisters, had flooded the shelter established by the Cosgrove Baptist Church right on the town square. The overflow was accepted by the United Methodist Church and Holy Cross Catholic. Christ the Savior Evangelical didn't actually have a permanent building, but they found three families each willing to take in one refugee woman in a pinch.

Her mother had told her that some other churchmen were

too afraid to get openly involved, but even some of this last group secretly contributed money or food. Stacey was surprised that Audrey, after a whole lifetime spent in impotent nattering, suddenly seemed to be coming alive. She now spent most of her days at the shelters, or introducing Stacey to the wide circle of women she seemed to know, coming back late and exhausted but always with a funny story to tell. Meanwhile, Don was so busy making the fake ankle bracelets during the day he had to hire a helper.

"Even if we do find a kidnapped woman, Dad, how are we going to get her back to Cosgrove?" This one-sided style of conversation seemed familiar. Her father had never been a talkative person. If he liked you, he'd fix your bike, paint your room, bandage your wounds. He just didn't believe in the power of talk. He would never make a politician. "Come on. Tell me what's going on."

"I got an extra bike stored at the place she's at."

"What place? For God's sake, Dad, just tell me."

"Reverend Ezekial's."

Of course. Reverend Ezekial, Frieda's idol, prophet, podcaster, inspirational leader of the Certainty Party. She remembered what Randy had said about the Genesis Riders. Their first plan had been to auction off the women on the internet. But the sheriff had intervened. The sheriff had insisted they do it the way set out in the Make Our Motherhood Strong bill. MOMS dictated that church leaders would decide where each woman would go. Reverend Ezekial was the richest and most famous and most outspoken church leader in Kansas. The Genesis Riders would obviously take the women to him first. And the first thing Ezekial would do would be to pick one for himself.

All Stacey needed was that one woman. She'd interviewed every one of the fugitives, but not one of them had actually been taken. And not one woman who had been taken had escaped.

Stacey needed a plaintiff for Roland's case who could say what actually was happening in Neola County. More importantly, she needed a witness to prove to all the people of Kansas the degradation all women would suffer if the Make Our Motherhood Strong Act were allowed to pass.

Ezekial's home church property was a large complex of brick buildings, including a huge three-story main church. It was way too late for services, but spotlights set on the wide surrounding lawns still illuminated the obligatory flagstone portico and the tall white columns. The electronic signboard read, in alternating colors: *The Reverend James Ezekial – God's word, the only word that counts.* They sped by quickly to avoid the light.

Reverend Ezekial had long since abandoned the modest little brick rancher right next door that had been used by all the previous ministers. He lived in a separate, gated community situated on a tiny little rise above the river, a development often mocked as "Alpine Acres" by the less fortunate townspeople. When they arrived, the gate was locked.

Don punched a number into the keypad and the gate swung open. Stacey wasn't surprised her father had figured out the code, but she asked anyway. "Simple video capture," he explained, as if she would immediately understand.

Behind the security booth and under a bush, there was a second cycle.

"I don't know how to drive one of these," Stacey whispered.

"Twist the handle to go. Brake pedal to stop. No gas motor to start up. No gears. No clutch. Infrared screen comes on automatically. You've driven a truck and a tractor. You've jumped a horse. This is a piece of cake by comparison."

They stashed both bikes there and stalked up the lane, stepping out of the light thrown by the lampposts at almost every door. A few doors up from the gate, a huge German Shepherd at the end of a chain growled and started barking, but

Don quickly threw out a large piece of raw steak he had been carrying in his bag for just such an occasion. The dog decided he wasn't so offended by their presence after all. They found Ezekial's house. Six or seven bedrooms, center hall, attached three-car garage, a deck to the side and, in back, a patio next to a pool edged in granite and surrounded by a smooth slate walkway that led to a cabana. No watchdog.

"Hubby and wife are supposed to be in Omaha tonight. We have time." There was a light on in the hallway downstairs and another in one of the bedrooms. The house undoubtedly had a security system, but Stacey was sure her father could disable it. "We have to check every room."

"No, we don't," Stacey whispered suddenly.

"What? Why do you say that?"

"He's been married for 15 years, and he's never had a concubine before."

"So?"

"Just think about it, Dad. No husband just says, 'Hi, honey. Oh, I got a new wife. Which bedroom do you think she should take?'"

"Not even Ezekial?"

"Not even Ezekial. Not for a while, anyway."

"So where do you put her in the meantime? Until Wifey the First accepts her new status?"

Stacey looked around. She suddenly felt certain. "In the cabana."

They tiptoed around the pool and onto the deck in front of the cabana, their footsteps drowned out by the barking of that same dog in the distance. Don took a pair of bolt cutters out of his bag and made short work of the padlock on the cabana door. There were no other locks. Stacey grabbed her father's hands and looked toward the eyes of his mask. She took a deep breath.

"Okay. Let's go in."

The flimsy cabana door creaked as they opened it. Don pushed her in and closed the door quickly behind them. It was pitch dark inside. Stacey reached for the mini-flashlight in her pocket.

"Who's there?"

The soft, tremulous voice startled her more than any scream could have. Stacey suppressed a yelp, but she was paralyzed.

"Who is it?"

Her father's voice was low and calm. "Friends. You're safe." He turned on his own flashlight but held his fingers over it so the light was not too harsh. "Were you kidnapped and brought here?"

"Yes."

"Are you hurt?"

"They tied me on a motorcycle and it burnt my legs. They still hurt. Reverend Ezekial said he'd get me to a doctor if it doesn't get better in a few days."

"Do you want to leave with us now?"

"He said I'm legally his property now."

"That's not true. Do you want to leave with us?"

"I'm chained to this hook in the floor."

Don found the chain with his flashlight and snapped it with the bolt cutters.

"Do you want to leave with us now?"

"Is this a test? He said the devil would test me."

Stacey thought a woman's voice would be more assuring. "Jesus wouldn't chain you to the floor and make you suffer those burns."

"How do I know that? I've been a sinner. Maybe Jesus is punishing me. The Reverend says I've been given a path of humility and service as a way to gain forgiveness."

"If the Reverend was doing Jesus's work, he wouldn't have to hide you from his wife and chain you in this shack."

Nobody spoke for a while. The dog could be heard barking

in the distance.

"I guess I would like to see a doctor."

"We'll take you to a doctor tonight. And in two days, if you want to come back here, we promise we'll bring you back."

They crept around the pool and alongside of the house, then took their masks off and tried to look casual as they walked down the curved roadway back toward the entrance gate. A car passed through the gate below. Don told them to keep walking, talking, looking at each other. Stacey found out a little about the girl's story. She wasn't pregnant and had never had a child. But she was the sister of an unmarried pregnant woman. Under Reverend Ezekial's strange logic, that alone put her in danger of falling into sin – and thus eligible to be taken in for training as a second wife.

The car coming up the lane slowed. It was highly unusual to see a person on foot in this neighborhood – but it would also be unusual for people here to recognize their neighbors. Stacey stared straight ahead and bobbed her head like she was listening to a tune on her phone. The car passed by and turned into a driveway up the hill, fortunately two or three doors past Ezekial's house. The German Shepherd barked again, this time in a way more curious than aggravated. Another piece of steak satisfied his curiosity. They finally reached the hidden bikes.

"What's your name?" Stacey's father whispered.

"Ruth."

"I'm Don. This is Stacey. I'm taking you to Cosgrove, and to a doctor. You have to ride on the back of my motorcycle. It's electric. There are no hot exhaust pipes." When the girl didn't respond, he went on. "It's about an hour ride. Are you strong enough to do that?"

"I guess."

Stacey could see her a little better now. The girl was taller than her, maybe five-nine. Short red pixie haircut. Strong chin. An older teenager, maybe seventeen or eighteen, long waist, broad shoulders. Naturally straight posture that was obvious as soon as the chain was cut off. But shaky now. "Have you had anything to eat today?"

"No. He said he would give me something, but he didn't." She still had the shackle on her wrist. "I can ride for an hour without eating. Thank you for doing this."

"We'll give you food as soon as we get there. Dad, am I supposed to ride the other cycle back behind you?"

"No."

*** ***

Speeding solo now under the moonless sky, guiding her cycle down the dark corridor indicated by the infrared screen, Stacey finally appreciated she was not in this fight alone. Her father had known where Kendrick was all along. Amy had been bringing food to him. They had felt they couldn't tell Stacey because she was his lawyer. They said Kendrick couldn't explain to anybody why he ran. But he had come out to the kids' gathering in the field because the urge to rap with his two friends had proven stronger than his fear. He had even cried when Amy told him the other kids wanted to hear him rap. When Amy told him later about the ankle bracelet demonstration at the fashion show, he had finally agreed to come back.

Unlike her father, Stacey had her license and was allowed to be out at night and to drive a regular car. But it was too dangerous for any young woman to be out at night in Neola County. It was too dangerous to carry her personal phone or any type of GPS device, but she had driven out to her father's old hideout room behind the record store more than a few times, months ago, to leave food for her father, and so she knew the way. Her father knew she had driven a bike and a car and a truck and a tractor and was an excellent horsewoman. He had told her an electric motorcycle was a piece of cake compared to any of those, and it turned out he was right. She just had to get used to looking at the screen instead of straight ahead.

No one ever took a trackable phone to Kendrick's hideout, and he was smart enough not to take one himself, so he was out of contact, and he couldn't know when anyone would come to pick him up. She imagined him lying on the sagging mattress in that decrepit room with the door locked, playing video games.

A shot of adrenaline ran through her when a line of single headlights, first on her screen and then in real life, barreled down on her from straight ahead. *Do not try to pull off the road once you see headlights*, her father had instructed her. *The last place they'll be looking for you is head-on.* Still, it took nerve to just power through straight forward. She twisted the accelerator to max as they passed, but she immediately realized this was a mistake. The rush of air from the other cycles almost pushed her off the road. They might not have seen her, but they must have felt that air pressure. She slowed and looked back. The line of taillights was swerving, and a few brake lights were lit. They seemed confused. She sped up.

The floodlights in front of the record store flared on her screen, and by the time she looked up she was already into the circle of light that spilled out onto the street. She turned quickly and went around to the back. She hadn't expected there would be anyone back there, and so she was shocked to see two guys sitting on lawn chairs set up on the ground underneath the second-floor landing. She cut the engine and coasted in the darkness to the far end of the lot. She held her breath as the tires silently rolled across the hard dirt plot but then crunched softly through the weeds. Stacey steered behind a bush near the back of the lot and stopped. The dim light from the bare bulb the men were sitting under didn't penetrate that far. But they both sat up and stared. Stacey froze, but it was clear they couldn't see anything. They were obviously addicts who lived in the other second-floor room. She couldn't see whether they were marked or not. They were sitting on the ground level, probably because the tiny second-floor landing wasn't big enough for their chairs plus the cooler they kept between them. There was a collection of empty beer bottles beside the cooler.

"Who's that? Fucking Riders!" The fatter of the two stood up and threw his beer in Stacey's direction, but the bottle fell way short. It didn't break but landed with a thud followed by a kind of exhausted fizz. He grabbed the other guy's bottle and began to throw it, but he was stopped by the other guy, who snatched his beer back.

"Jake, you asshole! We only got six left."

"Somebody's out there, Jake!"

"Don't get your panties in a bunch. The Riders don't hide in the bushes."

Stacey decided to wait the two Jakes out. Sweat was dripping down her neck inside the black hoodie, but she was determined not to move. But then her legs started trembling from holding that pose, and she knew she'd have to put the bike down soon. A car sped by on the road in front of the building, and she took advantage of the distraction to slowly put down her cycle and lie down behind it. She watched the glowing tips of the Jakes' cigarettes as they alternated between deep, slow drags and long gulps of beer. She wondered how long her father had been in that condition. She wondered if either of these two would ever be fully human again.

She heard the growl of motorcycles long before the two Jakes noticed. She wondered if she should warn the two men, but it was too dangerous to stand up. Besides, the riders probably hadn't seen her turn in behind the record store. They would probably just ride by. The fat Jake stood up.

"You hear it? You hear something *now*?"

The riders pulled to a rumbling, backfiring stop in front of the record store on the other side of the building. She could smell the exhaust, hear the yelling over the growling of the engines. She was sure they hadn't seen her turn in, but this was a logical place for her to be hiding. The two Jakes stood up to go up the stairs, but then they stopped and went back to pick up the remaining beer out of the cooler. Stacey shrunk back further into the bushes.

The engines suddenly roared into life, and Stacey saw headlight beams piercing the smoke and dust as they rounded the corner of the building. She counted seven sets of motorcycle headlights. The two addicts bumped into each other and dropped a beer bottle. It exploded on the cement. The lead rider stopped and shined a headlight in their faces. They looked confused. They didn't move. Their foreheads were branded.

"Zombies!" another rider yelled. The motorcyclists formed a semicircle around the two addicts and lit them up with their headlights.

"Hey guys. How you doing?" Fat Jake was trying to be cool, but another beer bottle slipped out of his arms and crashed on the cement.

"Pop the zombies! Pop the zombies!" The chant, and the ensuing laughter, could be heard even above the noise of the engines.

The leader pulled out a pistol and aimed. The two addicts cringed. Fat Jake got down on his knees. Tears glistened on his face in the bright lights. The leader motioned with his gun for skinny Jake to do the same. His body was shaking so badly he could hardly kneel. He dropped the rest of the bottles as he complied. A roar of laughter arose from the gang. The leader looked back at his gang and allowed a small smile to cross his face. He put the gun away. He led the rest of them around the building. The cycles roared and shot away up the road. Skinny Jake stood up, his knees still visibly shaking in the dim light from the bare bulb. The other Jake stayed kneeling as if stunned. They both stared down at the glass and foam from the broken beer bottles like they were considering lapping it up. Then, suddenly, a single motorcycle roared around the back of the house. The rider rose up and fired eight shots into fat Jake, then calmly slipped in a new clip and shot skinny Jake eight times as he tried to make his trembling way back up the stairs.

*** ***

Stacey pulled off her mask and gloves and stared at the house. Fat Jake was crumpled on the ground. Skinny Jake was splayed on the steps, sheets of glistening blood visible even in the dim light. There was no movement. Stacey flashed back to the Rider who had been killed in the field. The tide of blood was rising. She felt her gorge rising, but she had to swallow it down. She absolutely had to get Kendrick out now.

The light in Kendrick's room had been turned off. Stepping carefully to keep from touching the Jakes, she climbed the stairs. The door didn't open when she knocked.

"Kendrick, it's me, Stacey. You have to get out of here, *now*!" She shoved herself against the old wooden door, but it was solid. She stopped, waited.

The door opened. All she saw was the silvery muzzle of a gun pointing at her.

"It's me. It's just me, Stacey. There's nobody else here right now. Let me in. I've got to talk to you."

He let her in but didn't lower the gun. It was shaking in his hand.

"I know you're afraid, but we've got to go – now. I've got one of Dad's motorcycles. It's all planned. Nobody knows you ever left Cosgrove. Everybody covered for you there. But we've got to get out *right now*."

"Those shots?"

"Those guys who lived in the room next door. They're

both dead."

He followed her out, then stood watching as she tiptoed down the stairs and around the pools of blood that had seeped out from under the body of skinny Jake and were now congealing on the wooden steps. She looked back to see why he wasn't coming.

"You?" he called out hesitantly.

"What? Don't be afraid. But we have to get out of here."

"You shot them?"

How could he think that? Stacey tried to hold herself together. Had he learned not to trust anyone?

"No! No! The Genesis Riders did it. I saw it. If they find out we're here they'll come back to get us too."

Kendrick started to gag as he reached the bottom of the stairs. Stacey yanked him to the back of the yard so his puke would not leave his DNA anywhere the murder scene.

"It's awful, I know. But we have to get out of here now." They got on the bike and glided away to the soft whine of the engine. "You have to learn to figure out who your friends are, Kendrick."

"Nobody's my friend."

"The police still don't know you jumped bail. That's because Corinne covered for you. I'm going to be able to get your terrorism case dismissed. That's because I'm working on your case, and because Corinne is covering for you on that, too. Don't tell me you don't have friends."

"I wish I was dead." He was holding her tightly around the waist, his chin on her shoulder. He leaned his head hard into hers. She could feel his whole body trembling.

"You want to drive this thing?"

He did. He drove too fast, like she expected. But she was holding him tight from behind, and even as he veered back and forth across the center line she could feel his sudden laughter. A police car flashed by going the other way.

Chapter 27

If she be all tenderness, she will die.
– Nathaniel Hawthorne, *The Scarlet Letter*

Ruth had second degree burns on the calves of both legs. She was admitted to Cosgrove County General Hospital only as a precaution, and only after Roland had guaranteed payment. She was released the following day. By that time, Roland had already PDFd her affidavit and picture to the law school legal clinic, and the clinic filed a lawsuit asking for an injunction against the sheriff of Neola County.

Tall, wide-shouldered, with her pixie red hairdo and her habit of looking you straight in the eye, Ruth was the talk of this small town. This was not entirely a good thing, Stacey found out. Ruth didn't get along well with the other women refugees, most of whom actually were pregnant or had children out of wedlock. The publicity about Ruth's case had focused public attention on the church refugee center, and now a steady trickle of men was showing up at the door, some with offers of marriage for the women inside.

"Why don't you keep them away?" Stacey complained to her mother.

"It's a shelter, honey, not a concentration camp."

Stacey's name recognition was now at 82%, and 43% of likely voters said they'd probably vote for her. Stacey felt now that she could win. She simply told every women's group she talked to: *this could happen to you*. She told every man she met: *this could happen to your daughter*. She got heckled and jeered everywhere, and a shiver rode up her back every time she heard a motorcycle rumble near. Randy swore he could protect her, but his officers were also keeping an eye out at the church shelters, and his resources were being stretched thin.

A federal district court judge in Topeka granted the legal clinic's injunction, ordering Neola county sheriff Ned Weakins to enforce the laws against kidnapping, rape and unlawful imprisonment "unless and until MOMS becomes the law of the State of Kansas." Sheriff's Weakins then hired John "Dry Hole" Packer of PPD as his attorney. Packer immediately filed an appeal to a three-judge panel, filing the papers in person and bringing with him a crowd of about 30 men who orchestrated a chant just as the news cameras followed them to the courthouse door: *County rights/God's law*. But the three-judge panel did not seem to be in any hurry to decide the case.

*** ***

Corinne gave Kendrick back his ankle bracelet the day after Stacey brought him home. When she came to the door, Kendrick went out on the porch with her, and she just took it off and handed it to him. They didn't seem to be talking. Stacey had planned much more of a thank-you ceremony for the little girl she had come to admire. But Corinne was already turning to go as Stacey came outside.

"Corinne," she called, and the teenager turned back. "We owe you so much. My mother made this for you. To thank you."

Corinne didn't seem particularly happy. She stood with one hand on her hip and the other brushing back her thick hair from her eyes – exposing the "what now?" expression that suddenly crossed that long, angular face. She had given Stacey a sworn affidavit that might help get the terrorism case against Kendrick dismissed. She swore in that affidavit that she had never been pregnant. By signing that affidavit, Corinne had probably saved Kendrick from spending his entire youth in jail. Stacey wondered if it was a lie. She was now just hoping Corinne would have the guts to repeat her story before the prosecutor. Stacey had to rely on hope now because she had no choice but to trust Corinne. The whole family was grateful, and they needed to show it. Stacey handed her a beautiful jeweled cell phone holder made by the women in the shelter. It was in the style of an ankle bracelet.

"Oh. Thank you."

"Honey" – Stacey caught herself using her mother's word – "Kendrick's out on bail now because of you. We're going to get the case dismissed because of you. We all owe you so much."

Corinne looked skeptical, meeting Stacey's eyes with her own green-eyed stare. "I guess it was all my fault to begin with."

Stacey had to stop herself from pushing her brother from behind. *Give the girl a fucking hug, for Christ's sake.*

"Thank you," he managed.

Corinne looked him up and down. He had grown another inch and was now half a foot taller than she was. She looked impressed. But she seemed to realize that if she wanted anything to happen between them, she'd have to start it herself. Both hands in her pockets now, Corinne met Stacey's eyes, then Kendrick's, worked her jaw slowly, then nodded, then turned and walked away.

"That's one great girl. You should go after her."

"I know."

*** ***

Ruth was not happy at the shelter. The other women, one by one, kept asking her about her pregnancy, but she wasn't pregnant. A lot of the male visitors wanted to talk to her first. News people wanted her story. She seemed afraid to jeopardize her sister, who actually was pregnant and who had been taken somewhere else the night they were kidnapped. Her father reached her on the phone one day at the shelter. When she walked into Audrey's house that night, she looked confused. "He said come back. Don't fight God's will."

"They can take your sister's baby as soon as it's born." Stacey conjured up the worst possible scenario. "If it's a girl, they can have somebody else raise her, or just sell her as a concubine. They can chain your sister up like they did to you. Turn her into an unpaid servant. Change her name."

"But she *has* sinned."

"So have I." Stacey had her attention. "But I still think I have the right to be free, to keep my baby, to marry whoever I want." But Stacey still couldn't convince her that Reverend Ezekial wasn't receiving his instructions directly from God. She asked Audrey for help.

"Bring her into our home," Audrey told her. "I'll give her your Dad's old den to sleep in." She shrugged. "House'll be crowded. Oh well."

Chapter 28

They were sick of meeting in the bed and breakfast. The charm was gone, and neither of them had the extra time in their day for the drive there and back. Roland officially moved out of the apartment he had lived in with Frieda. He found a corner apartment on the third floor of a new apartment complex a short distance outside of Topeka.

"This is my new home, and also my legislative office."

"Hmm. Nothing in here yet but a bed."

"Hmm."

They inaugurated the new bed. Afterwards he lay on his back, staring at the ceiling. She was lying next to him, her arm and her leg thrown over him as if still trying to possess him.

"This is what I live for, Stacey. Being with you."

"I love it, too."

"You're my only real family, Stacey. I've never had that before. But I want all of you."

"What do you mean? You have all of me."

He sat up and reached into his backpack on the floor beside the bed. He pulled out something and handed it to her. It was another postcard from Grant.

"That's why this thing with Grant bothers me so much."

"Another postcard? I can't stop him from sending postcards."

"It says *thanks for your kind letter*."

"Oh. Well. His company gave a huge donation to my campaign. And they're sending their best IT guy to set up a voter identification project."

"You wrote to him."

"I added a couple of sentences at the bottom of a form letter. That's all." Stacey sat up and slipped into her underwear. There wouldn't be any second go-rounds today, she realized.

But she was wrong. The second round came when they

were outside on his tiny concrete balcony. He came at her from behind when she was leaning on the iron rail, listening to the leaves sighing in the cottonwoods in the field next door.

"Ooh! You like outdoor fun," she teased. Stacey would not be outdone by anyone when it came to sex. Still, he was a little too fast this time, and afterwards he just stood silently in the far corner of the balcony, sipping a glass of bourbon he had poured just for himself.

"I get angry sometimes," he confessed. She went inside and poured her own drink, but then she remembered she was pregnant. She left the glass on the counter and came out to confront him. He spoke first. "I'm finally becoming my own person, getting my independence from Golsch."

"Finding your own political conscience."

"Yes. But then something like this ... this *Grant thing* happens, and I see you're not really on my side."

"Of course, I'm on your side." She started to walk closer to comfort him, but he held his hand against her chest, keeping her away. His eyes were cold.

"Sometimes I think you're playing both sides of the street between me and Grant."

She called Grant later that day to tell him not to send her any more postcards.

"So, I can't communicate with you any way at all."

"Those postcards are delivered practically straight to my boyfriend. I didn't even get to read your last one. What did it say?"

They started talking. She told him Roland knew she was pregnant and was going to help her raise the child.

"Is he going to marry you?"

"We're sort of engaged."

He let it drop without asking for any more details – let it drop like a good ex-boyfriend should. She asked him if Lacee had signed a CTS form for him. He said she had. She wanted to ask if Lacee was as good in bed as she was but decided to play the good ex-girlfriend role herself. She didn't ask him anything else about Lacee. He said Liotech wanted him to check with Stacey every once in a while to see how the IT guy was doing on her campaign.

"Oh. I guess that would be okay."

"Good."

"So, um, goodbye."

"Stacey."

"What?"

"Boy or girl?"

"Um, girl. Not that you have any right to know."

"Stacey, I panicked and made a terrible mistake."

"You sure did." She hung up.

Chapter 29

Reverend James Ezekial appeared on WKTK, Cosgrove's only television station. His first wife must have heard about Ruth by now, because Ezekial was no longer trying to hide that he'd taken her. "I want my wife back!" he shouted out from the screen. "My, wife Ruth, who was kidnapped under cover of darkness by evil secularists who believe that man's law is above the law of God. And now Randy Crenshaw, the Sheriff of Cosgrove County, is aiding her kidnappers and defying God's will. It is God's will that I be reunited with my God-given helpmeet."

"Turn that off!" Audrey screamed. "I don't want Ruth hearing that." But Stacey just turned it down and sat closer to the screen.

"The Sheriff of Cosgrove County is allowing Stacey Davenport to harbor not only my God-given wife but also 27 other women whom God has promised to other good men who will help reform these poor lost souls with love and patience and discipline. *Wives, submit to your husbands as to the Lord.* Ephesians 5:22.

"The law of Kansas hasn't caught up to the law of God yet, but I call on all able-bodied Christians to retrieve these women, this flock of 27 wayward women, from Ms. Davenport, that handmaid of the devil, who now holds them in captivity in Cosgrove."

The television station switched to a commercial.

Stacey sighed. "At least he's admitting what he's doing is illegal."

"At least he didn't say exactly where the women are," Audrey added.

The news anchor returned. "The women the Reverend Ezekial is referring to have fled Neola county, apparently voluntarily, and they tell us they left because they were afraid of being taken and assigned as second wives to husbands not of their own choosing. Stacey Davenport, a law student and local candidate in the special election for the legislative seat formerly held by Baldwin Touhey, tells WKTK news that the "kidnapping and concubinage," as she calls it, is of course illegal now. She alleges, however, such crimes will become perfectly legal if MOMS passes."

"Oh, that's great! That's exactly the kind of information that needs to get out there to the voters." Audrey was exhilarated.

"The women are being housed in the Cosgrove Baptist Church hall on the corner of Pleasant Street and Harding Road, right on the town square in Cosgrove."

*** ***

Stacey called WKTK and demanded equal time. Roland laughed at this. "Don't you know what the FCC is doing to equal time? Equal time now means that the stockholders of a broadcast company have access equal to the value of their investment. It means the point of view of the hyper-wealthy, like the Golsch brothers, gets pounded into the heads of citizens day after day. That's why Robert Golsch was so set on controlling the FCC."

"What's that got to do with me? I'm just talking about fairness. In Kansas, we still believe in fairness."

The station manager, Bill Henderson, did believe in fairness but, to be safe, he checked first with Robert Golsch. Golsch was way too high a personage to be called directly by a lowly station manager, so the contact was arranged through Roland. Roland brought Stacey along. "I talked with Mr. Golsch," he told Henderson. "Mr. Golsch would be happy if you let Ms. Davenport reply on the air." Stacey's mouth dropped open as she watched Roland so smoothly lie.

"Golsch will never notice," he explained to Stacey later in the car. "There's no love lost between him and Reverend Ezekial anyway. Robert actually hates the CP. He funds their campaigns, and he lets them enact all the religious crap into law they want – but it's just so they'll pass whatever legislation is good for his bank account."

*** ***

"None of these women currently being sheltered in Cosgrove were kidnapped," Stacey began her televised statement. "Twelve of them drove here on their own because of what is happening in Neola County. Nine more called into their church for help, and their minister put them in contact with the shelter, and the women made their own arrangements to come here. Six were brought here by boyfriends who were afraid of losing their children.

"And let me tell you about the last woman we rescued. She was found chained to a post in a shed behind the house of her new owner. She had been given no food or water for over 24 hours. She had untreated second degree burns on her legs. She left voluntarily and was taken first to Cosgrove County General, where they kept her overnight. Then she came to the shelter. She has since moved, and she is now in another safe place in Cosgrove County.

"Her new owner who treated her so badly was the Reverend James Ezekial. James Ezekial came on this show yesterday and claimed that she is his wife and she was kidnapped. She's not his wife. They were never married. In any case, it's still illegal to have more than one wife in Kansas, and Ezekial already has a wife. So almost everything he told you yesterday on this show was a lie.

"But one really important thing he told you was true. If the bill proposed by the Certainty Party called MOMS passes, everything he did to her will be made legal. It will be legal to take her by force from her parents and to assign her as someone's second wife. That man can change her name, forbid her any contact with the outside world, punish her severely if she disobeys. She will be his property. He will own any female children she gives birth to.

"This might be our last chance to keep this from happening to our own daughters. Please go to the polls. Please vote. Please let our women stay free."

Stacey was thrilled that the news anchor let her finish her spiel, but she was surprised at the first question.

"Miss Davenport, you have now admitted publicly that you are pregnant. How does the outcome of this race affect your personal situation?"

"A lot. As you know, I can't leave Kansas while pregnant, thanks to Conception Control. So I have to stay here. And of course, every time I go to the doctor, I have to be accompanied by a Conception Control officer. But I want to emphasize that it can get much worse. If MOMS passes, law enforcement will come and get me and take me away, and I'll be assigned by a local churchman to be someone's concubine."

"That must be a frightening prospect."

"I am afraid. I'm scared. I've met Reverend Ezekial, and he already hinted he would take me as his personal concubine."

Stacey was exhausted. She didn't like to experience this fear in her heart, much less talk about it publicly. But she was glad she admitted it. The anchorwoman, however, was not finished.

"Given these heart-shattering risks you are taking here in Kansas, I wonder why you didn't just stay in Massachusetts when you first found out you were pregnant?"

Stacey's mouth dropped open. Was this really anybody's business? How did she know this, anyway? Roland had told her that politics was dirty pool, and to expect anything.

"I love Kansas. My family has been here for five generations. I was in my third year of law school here. I wanted to be a lawyer here – when that was still legal."

"But – the father? I assume you had a close relationship with him?"

"I did. We talked about marriage." How much more would she have to reveal?

"But you two ultimately decided not to marry?"

"We ...." That first word out was a lie. There hadn't been any *we*. "We decided I couldn't abandon Kansas and my career. And he couldn't abandon his career in Massachusetts and live under the Certainty Party's rules in Kansas."

"So, you two decided together that your careers, in the end, were more important than marriage?"

He stood me up, she wanted to shout. This "career" talk sounded so cold compared to the hot anger and disappointment she felt that afternoon in Boston when Grant told her he wasn't ready to marry her and be a father to her child. Up until that instant, she had thought he was the ideal man who would jump at the chance to marry her and raise their baby. Then, when she saw the shock on his face, she blamed herself for being too idealistic and rigid, and she tried to compromise. Then he ran out anyway.

"No, it wasn't careers," she answered. "It was just a star-crossed love, in every way. I hope you won't ask me any more of these deeply painful, personal questions. Just know that I love Kansas and I want to keep it from turning into something horrible."

Chapter 30

Kendrick was alarmingly blasé about the charges against him. He seemed only mildly interested when she told him she and Harshaw had moved to get the charges dismissed. Corinne's affidavit said she had never been pregnant, but that her sister was in Maryland looking into alternate methods of fertilization, which were illegal in Kansas, and she was looking on the internet just to see what that was all about. The prosecutor, faced with Corinne's affidavit, and Kendrick's silence, and the minimal computer evidence the police had collected, still demanded a face to face meeting with Corinne before he would even think about dismissing the charges. On the way to the meeting Stacey told her as much as she could about the conception laws in Kansas. Then she just crossed her fingers and hoped Corinne's story would hold together.

"So, you were looking up information about *in vitro* fertilization because you were thinking about getting pregnant that way." The prosecutor, Richard Cory, a tired-looking man with a sour grimace on his face, began the interrogation without even introducing himself.

It was a trick question. Stacey had explained to Corinne that in the process of *in vitro* fertilization, more than one egg was often fertilized, and once a few were successfully implanted the rest were usually discarded. According to the Feto-Terrorism law, each one of those discarded eggs would count as a murder.

"You're kidding," Corinne answered the prosecutor.

"No, I'm not kidding. Kendrick was helping you to look into undergoing *in vitro*, wasn't he?"

Corrine's answer to the prosecutor's question was quick – and forceful in a flat, offhand way. "No, I wasn't thinking about getting pregnant that way."

Prosecutor Cory jumped in fast. "And that's because you

were already pregnant, right?"

Corinne looked at him, her lips pressed together in a thin line. "No, I was never pregnant. Didn't you read the paper I signed?"

"You don't really have a sister in Maryland who is undergoing *in vitro*, do you?" he practically shouted. It was more of a statement than a question – as if he were cross-examining her.

"You want me to get her on the phone?" Corinne looked exasperated.

"She's waiting at the phone right now, if you want to call her," Stacey chimed in.

They were well prepared. The prosecutor's look grew even more sour. "I could charge both Kendrick and you with helping your sister commit Feto-Terrorism." But he was practically mumbling by this time. Stacey guessed he didn't have the energy for a knock-down legal fight.

"Maybe you could charge them, but you couldn't convict them. There's no evidence that she or Kendrick were helping her sister do anything. And I can guarantee you they'll all testify they weren't." Stacey was amazed at her own audacity. But she couldn't stop. "If you don't dismiss this case, I guarantee you the trial will be an embarrassment to your office and the state." She hesitated long enough for that to sink in. Then she hit him where she thought it would really hurt. "And Reverend Ezekial and the Certainty Party will know you are bungling the enforcement of their new laws."

Cory asked them to wait outside. Harshaw, Kendrick's official lawyer, hadn't said a word in the meeting. Stacey now asked him what he thought.

"I think that little girl just saved your brother," Harshaw murmured, and smiled. "But I didn't believe a word she said."

Stacey leaned in closer to him and kept her voice low. "Yeah. I still don't know exactly what the truth is."

The heavy wooden door to the prosecutor's office opened

suddenly, and his office assistant came out. "Prosecutor Cory will not be coming out here himself. But he sent me out here to tell you the charges will be dismissed."

*** ***

When the charges against him were dismissed, Kendrick didn't have to act like he was public enemy number one any more. Kids in school started calling him "Ankle Bracelet Man," but in a good way. He connected again with Pete and Jeremy as best he could. Pete was obsessed with playing high school football next year and spent most of his weekends practicing football, but they managed to talk a little on weekdays. Jeremy never mentioned a thing about getting Corinne pregnant, and he never said anything about the trouble Kendrick had been in or how he got out of it. He said he wasn't with Corinne any more. Kendrick got both Pete and Jeremy to go to a small outdoor meeting one night where he rapped without a microphone in front of about ten kids in a field. Corinne wasn't there.

He took his father's bike one night to visit Corinne. He knew her parents weren't home. He broke his no-cell-calls rule and texted her that he wanted to come over. All she replied was "when?" At her house, he hid the bike behind a bush and left his mask and gloves in the saddlebags. He knew he wasn't a criminal any more, but he still felt like he had to act like one. The two small windows on either side of the portico at her front door glowed with a dim light. He paused and took a deep breath before he rang the doorbell.

She didn't have any fancy clothes or makeup on. Her skinny legs looked lost in her shorts. She had on a white blouse. He thought it looked like she might be growing some breasts since the last time he saw her. She was still fighting a losing battle wrestling with all that hair.

"Yeah?" was all she said. But her green eyes seemed softer

now. Corinne had never been a cheery, smiley person. She was the kind of person who would always let you know exactly what she thought. About anything, including yourself. She waved him in and closed the door behind him.

"There's a lot of stuff I don't know about what happened," he blurted out.

"Me too."

Inside, the house was stuffy and hot. She led him to a side porch, where they sat together on a clanky aluminum double recliner. He could feel a light breeze here. She left the top light on, but there were shadows.

"You go first," she said.

"I can't believe ...." He stumbled. "I can't believe that you could have actually, um, had a baby."

"It's a characteristic of all females," she said evenly.

He liked the way she talked. It made him want to forge on. None of the women in his house ever talked about any of this stuff around him. He hoped she would go on and answer the rest of his questions before he even asked them, but she didn't. She raised her head a little, and he could see her steady eyes in the new light.

"So? Are you pregnant?"

"No."

"Did, um, were you pregnant *before*?"

"No. It was a false alarm."

He didn't know what a false alarm was. She explained it to him. There was a long silence while he shifted around and the plastic cushions squeaked on the aluminum frames.

"What was that weird stuff we were looking at on my computer?"

"*In vitro*. It's for people who can't get pregnant the regular way."

"Why were we looking at that?"

"I don't know. My sister couldn't get pregnant. She was

166

trying to get pregnant *in vitro* in Maryland. Maryland's a blue state. It's legal there. It's like a test tube thing, the sperm and the eggs swimming around in a bowl or something."

"Woo. Weird shit."

"It was all my fault," she said. She kept pulling her hair back with one hand so her face was in the light as she talked. "I knew it was dangerous to look up stuff like that on the internet. I'm the one who made you do it. It was my fault you got arrested. You were just trying to be nice to me. I'm sorry."

"But you saved my ass with that ankle bracelet thing."

"I wasn't going to let you get arrested again."

"That was really great. I didn't know girls could be brave like that."

He was glad her face was in shadow again and he couldn't see her reaction. But what he said was true, so who cared? "I hate being back in school."

"You can catch up."

"No. I mean, I was such a dick to everybody."

"You were always nice to me."

She grabbed a thick swath of her hair and half hid behind it. He leaned in. "Can't I see your whole face?"

"It's funny looking, I know." But she took both hands and swept her hair up and away.

"No, it's not. It's pretty."

Her eyes were steady. "I think you want to kiss me."

The thought hadn't crossed his mind. But then it did. He wondered what kissing her would be like. But he didn't have to wonder. So he did it, right then.

They reclined the chair a few more notches and kissed again. He was so excited he forgot his embarrassment over his hard-on. She looked only at his face, put her hand only on his shoulder. They seemed to be practicing kissing.

"Did you … with Jeremy … a lot?"

"Only once."

"Did you like it?"

"No."

She didn't seem to want him to do it right then. He was glad of that. He really didn't know how. Those internet women didn't seem real like Corinne. This was a different thing.

"How about if I ride my bike over here early tomorrow and we ride the school bus together."

"Okay."

Chapter 31

"Do you really think we should do this now? I mean, I should leave right now if I want to make that meeting at the shelter in Cosgrove." Stacey and Roland had slept the night together in Roland's Topeka apartment. Just slept.

"We didn't make love last night." Roland flashed her an aggravated look with suddenly suspicious blue eyes.

"I know. The first time ever. Not a good thing, I guess. When I got in from the rally it was after midnight and you were already asleep."

"You didn't think I'd want you to wake me up?" His tone was accusatory.

"I didn't know. Honestly, I was tired myself."

"You'd just as soon skip making love to me?"

"I didn't say that. Really, can't you tell I want to have sex with you all the time?"

"Prove it to me, now."

She did. He was gentle, but he took his time. Something she would have savored any other day, and for a few moments she completely forgot about the meeting at the shelter. But afterwards, lying together with him, she started wondering if she could still get to Cosgrove if she jumped up now and drove 90 the whole way. But she was afraid to rush out.

He did love her, and she was afraid to hurt his feelings. He seemed so sensitive since he lost the patronage of Golsch – and after his mother blamed him for that. Stacey understood what it was like to have all the people who nurtured and supported you your whole life suddenly doubting you. She knew it was awful. He needed her more than ever. He loved her, and he was spending all his energy to get her elected. And he wanted to raise her child. He was worth missing one little meeting.

It seemed he held her for a really long time, until it was

utterly impossible for her to make it to Cosgrove. She sighed, laid her head on his chest and dreamed of a day when the world wouldn't be in such constant turmoil. But when she finally pulled away, he surprised her.

"Why did you protect Grant in that interview on WKTK?" he spoke from the bed, his voice gruff.

"What do you mean?"

"You know what I mean."

"When that interviewer asked why Grant and I didn't get married? I said I came back here because I love Kansas."

Back in Boston, when she had first told Grant she was pregnant, he had frozen, then stood up, staggered backwards, started pacing with a panicked look on his face. She had known it would be a shock, but when he didn't show any signs of recovering for long minutes, and didn't even make eye contact with her, she saw that his basic reaction was fear. Being from a broken family with an addicted father and a long history of addiction herself, she had lived a lifetime feeling like an outsider. Grant had helped her believe in herself, but his panic when she offered herself to him had only confirmed her deepest fears.

"I thought it was a good answer," she told Roland now. "I thought I did a good job kind of mushing over the whole thing."

"You didn't tell the truth."

She hadn't told the whole truth. The whole truth was she had caved. She had told him she would marry him and stay in Massachusetts, give up her law degree and her career plans – and especially her dream of rising to a position where she could reach back and repay her family for her sins against it. She had offered up all her dreams and plans if Grant would marry her and be a father to her child. But he had just stared at her, silent, white-faced, shaking – before he ran out.

"The truth is, the only reason you didn't marry him was because he abandoned you. Why didn't you tell the truth?"

"I ... I ...."

"He abandoned you. That's the truth. And that's something people can understand. It would have helped your campaign. But you didn't say it. And I think I know why you didn't say it."

"You tell me. Why didn't I say it?" Her voice was brittle.

"You didn't say it because you didn't want to make Grant look bad, like the scum that he is. You put his reputation above the good of our campaign."

"Okay, I didn't want to hurt him. But he's helping our campaign. A lot. Look, the Golsch money has dried up. Because of you. Because you stuck to your principles and defied even the rest of the Independents and refused to vote to override the veto of the Professional Reformation Act. I admire you for that. I really do. But now we don't have Golsch, and we need Grant's company's help even more now."

Still lying on the bed, he spoke to her as she hurried into her clothes. "Politics. You're saying you're taking Grant's help just because you need it in your campaign. If I halfway believed that, we wouldn't be having this argument."

* * * * * *

Grant announced he was moving to Kansas for the remainder of the campaign. To make matters even stickier, he arrived in Cosgrove soon afterward, then spent a lot of time at the shelter and at Stacey's mother's house. Audrey had always liked Grant, and she seemed to lean on him for support when Don disappeared, as he usually did during the daylight hours. Then Grant surprised everybody by deciding that Ruth needed a bodyguard and by assigning that job to himself. He even bought a revolver and carried it awkwardly in a shoulder holster under his suitcoat, much to the amusement of the whole town. He also encouraged Ruth to make friends with the dog, Shelbie. He did it for her protection, but she took naturally to the dog, and soon he was following her everywhere. Grant was busy most days helping Audrey schedule events for Stacey or setting up canvassing routes or conducting orientation meetings for volunteers, but he talked to Ruth a lot whenever he was in the house.

Grant seemed to be the only person in Cosgrove who could get through to Ruth. He was probably not like any man Ruth had ever met before. Ruth, tall, lean, broad-shouldered, plainspoken but quiet, still seemed confused about what had happened to her. She cornered Audrey in the kitchen one day.

"But the Bible says men can have many wives and concubines. *Wives, submit to your husbands, as it is fitting in the Lord.* Isn't the Bible telling me to go back to Reverend Ezekial?"

"Honey, it also says, *Slaves, submit yourself to your masters.* You believe that?"

"I don't know what that passage means. I would have to ask somebody."

"Who would you ask? That's the question, isn't it? Reverend Ezekial? Can't you tell he's interpreting the Bible just out of his own sick fantasies?"

Ruth's confusion over religious issues seemed to be keeping her from feeling any solidarity with any of the women in the shelter – or with Stacey or Audrey or Amy, for that matter. Her father called them all Jezebels whenever she talked to him on the phone. She seemed like a ghost in the house from another millennium. When Randy talked with her about her kidnapping, she listened, but even Randy treated her cagily, like a witness who might go bad on the witness stand. Don's off-and-on presence around the house – and his lack of a job – disqualified him from being the kind of father figure she could relate to.

Grant was just a little taller than Ruth, handsome, well-dressed, well-spoken, and he now carried a gun. Ruth didn't seem to notice that he didn't know how to use it. Grant seemed to understand that she was confused about the more complicated world she was now living in, and he seemed happy to try to explain it to her. She seemed to trust him. He was sophisticated and exotic to her; she couldn't easily categorize him – and thus she couldn't mention him to her father. She listened to him like a person from a totally different planet whom she had to treat with respect. But nobody realized the extent of his influence until she herself was interviewed on WKTK.

"I don't know what to believe any more," she answered the reporter's first question. "They're holding my sister Renee somewhere in Neola County. She hasn't been allowed to contact anybody in our family. She's twenty-one. Renee and her boyfriend were going to get married next month." She looked right at the camera and brushed her short, red, pixie-styled hair back with both hands as if she needed to. "Now they're forcing her to be some other man's wife. I don't know everything, but I know in my heart that's not right."

"But isn't your sister a fallen woman?"

"I don't know. But I know she's a lot better person than I am. There couldn't be a kinder, sweeter person than Renee." The camera focused on the tears filling her eyes, pooling, then running down her face as she held her head still and didn't even try to wipe them away. "What they're doing to her, it's just not right."

*** ***

"How's your new girlfriend, Ruth?" Stacey had just pulled up at the house, her back seat full of signs she hadn't been able to convince any farmers to put in the corners of their fields. They were pretty small, and they couldn't compete with the giant signs that Bradford Bullins, the CP candidate, had erected on all the main roads leading out of town. The signs showed God's eye as it appeared on the back of a one-dollar bill and the simple slogan: *A vote CP is a vote for Me.* Smaller signs dotted almost every mile of every road in the county, each with the same simple message: *God and MOMS*. But Stacey's name recognition was now 92%, thanks in part to Ezekial's harangue on WKTK and Stacey's rebuttal. Roland had told her the signs weren't as important now and she should concentrate on walking the streets and stores and talking to anybody she could. Almost half the people turned away or snubbed her, and a lot of the men openly called her a junkie or a whore, but the latest poll showed her winning the support of 55% of the likely voters. All they had to do was just keep things going as they were.

"My *girlfriend*? Very funny." Grant helped her carry the signs back into the house. "Ruth's a very intelligent, level headed girl. It's just that the world she comes from is so small."

"She looked really strong on TV. But every time she calls her father, she thinks she should go back to being Ezekial's concubine."

"I don't think she can really distinguish her father from God yet." He reached into the trunk to grab some of the signs for her. "And her father can't distinguish himself from God either, from what I can tell," he laughed.

She laughed, too. "So, how do you get her to talk to you about that kind of stuff?"

"For starters, I'm a guy," he smiled. "And I'm from a different world. She's smart, and she's curious about that world."

She watched him carry all the signs into her mother's house. She was due to meet and greet people on the street in Orwell, a town even smaller than Cosgrove. Roland was already there doing the advance work, which in this case consisted of getting permission to set up a table on the sidewalk. But she hesitated before she got back into the car. She was trying to figure out her own feelings about Grant. She knew that in his quiet, modest way he could sweep Ruth off her feet if he wanted to. But she didn't think he would. She believed he was really one of the good guys, even in his personal life. She knew her campaign would have stumbled off track by now if he and Liotech hadn't come to help. But she still didn't quite understand where his head was at. She wished she could find out. After a few minutes she realized she was standing next to the car, waiting for him – but he wasn't coming back out.

*** ***

"I still don't get why we had to look up that weird stuff on the internet."

Kendrick and Corinne were talking quietly in the back of the bus. They had only one class together, but they rode the bus together every day. On the bus, she talked with everyone else, too, but they found ways to talk alone. They hadn't talked about the Feto-Terrorism case since that first night on her parents' porch.

"I wanted to know about what was happening to my sister. The test tubes and shit."

"You could have just called her up."

"It was really embarrassing. How ignorant I was. I didn't want to talk to her yet."

"Yet?"

"Um, what I was thinking – I mean, this is so, so dumb. What I was thinking was if I really was pregnant, maybe I could somehow, um, I don't know, give the baby to her ... in a test tube or something. Don't laugh."

He wasn't laughing.

She went on. "And I got you in so much danger by my stupid plan. I'm really sorry."

"It wasn't a stupid plan." No, it wasn't a stupid plan. She wasn't stupid. She was a really smart person. And a really nice one. One you could always count on. And she seemed to just naturally like him. He decided right then that he would never have to look any further. She would do.

The large gatherings of kids petered out after the Genesis Riders' attack. Every kid questioned by Randy denied being there or knowing the names of any other kids who had been there. The police got zero worthwhile information, even from Corinne, who had just barely escaped. Nothing went on social media about it. Law enforcement and all the other officials who ran the lives of children were totally blacked out by the kids. The blackout extended to parents. The kids now acted as if nothing good could ever come from telling anybody anything.

Kendrick and Corinne tried to tell the truth to each other. Kendrick said he'd die for his father or Stacey but he didn't care much about anybody else. Corinne included him on her list. He decided his list should be a little longer, too. When he was with her, the outside world didn't seem so confusing. They kissed passionately when they had a chance, but neither of them tried to go any further.

"You could've been killed that night." He was talking about the night the bikers crashed the gathering of kids in the field. "I saw that one biker swinging his chain at you."

"I was really scared. But everybody's scared now. Some kids in my class were talking. They said the police have a video of the fashion show, and they're coming to school soon to arrest everyone who wore an ankle bracelet or a fake mark on their forehead. They're saying they'll all be sent to a rehabilitation camp."

Chapter 32

An effigy of a very pregnant witch, with devil's horns poking through her hat, hung from a rope strung between two telephone poles across the main shopping street in Orwell.

"Oh, cool. I'm going to pose right next to it."

"Absolutely not!" Roland ordered. "Politics is a game of symbols. People don't think in sentences. They think in symbols. The last thing we want to do is publicize the other side's symbol."

Stacey obeyed. He was probably right. If she stood next to it, that would practically force all the media in the state to publicize the effigy – and the effigy, and not the story behind it, would get all the attention. The point of the rally was to get her own message across. But she didn't like the way he yelled at her.

Grant had arrived late and was helping set up for the rally, too. She didn't like the look that came into his eyes when Roland yelled at her. The last thing she needed now was for those two guys to start fighting.

The election was in three weeks. Her percentage had slipped 1%, which was a dip less than the margin of error, but that was still worrisome. The important thing at this point was to get people to notice there was an election and to believe that the results would make a difference in their lives. She was used to being called a slut and a whore, but now there was a new chant going around, this one about her projected downfall:

Stacey –
Spread your legs, save your life,
Be the prophet's second wife.

These insults just made her more determined to sound

like the reasonable candidate. But it seemed like other things were coming apart at the seams. Ruth had clearly fallen in love with Grant, and Stacey and Grant had argued about it. Stacey thought Ruth had just pathetically transferred all her father-worship to a new man and that Grant shouldn't encourage it. He promised he was only trying to get her to think for herself.

Roland now was complicating everything, insisting on reading all of Stacey's speeches ahead of time. This was slowing down every appearance. And he always castigated her later if she went off script.

They were sitting at a folding table in a vacant lot rented from a used car dealer across the street. The dealer had rented the lot to her for the afternoon for only $50. He had even sent over his lot man to clean up the litter and debris.

"Boy, he must really like you," Grant remarked.

Stacey shook her head at his ignorance. "He's never heard of me, Grant. This is Kansas. People are nice."

This is what they called the "tiny table" method. Stacey used it only if they couldn't locate a single supporter to actually host a little meeting of politically interested people. It had worked in a few of the smaller towns. It worked even better if some of the nastier supporters of Bradford Bullins, the CP candidate, showed up and screamed obscenities at her. They would call the police as soon as the catcalls got too obscene, a patrol car would cruise by, the obscenities would get worse, and the cat-caller would be moved along. Stacey would stand behind the table, a dignified but slightly hurt look on her face. As soon as the first person came up to sympathize, the ice would be broken. Stacey would talk quietly, smile gamely and shrug her shoulders, and a little stream of people would edge by to get the same treatment. Stacey was always surprised at the number of people who had no idea what was going on in Kansas – and who didn't want to believe her when she told them what was happening right now in neighboring Neola County. She sometimes thought the whole campaign was worth it if she could get people just to pay attention to what was happening. None of it would matter, of course, if the Certainty Party managed to overturn the governor's veto of MOMS. Would she really be forced to become Ezekial's concubine? Wasn't there some corner of Kansas she could flee to?

A lot of people told her which church they belonged to, and Stacey began to develop a shortcut for identifying potential supporters. "It doesn't matter what actual denomination they belong to. If they say they are God-fearing, they'll hate me. If they talk about Jesus, I have a chance."

It didn't hurt with the women passing by that Grant was sitting on one side the table and Roland on the other. A few asked for Roland's autograph when they found out he was already a delegate. It was mostly just an excuse to talk to such a fantastically handsome guy. Others seemed impressed that a handsome Boston lawyer would think it was worth his time to sit in a vacant lot in Orwell and talk to them. The dynamic male duo was doing well, but she could see how badly Roland was resenting Grant's presence.

Grant took a call on his phone that made him drop his chat with a sixty-year-old lady who was describing the medical conditions of her three cats. He rushed over and spoke in Stacey's ear. "WKTK fired Bill Henderson, the station manager."

"What? Why?"

"For letting you and Ruth talk on the air, of course. The publicity from those interviews is what's keeping your campaign afloat. Golsch controls that station, you know."

She couldn't help but turn accusingly toward Roland. "Golsch got Henderson fired? Did you know about that?"

"No." He looked hurt. Then he lowered his voice so Grant couldn't hear. "But I'm not surprised. Golsch thinks I betrayed him. I'm on my own now. And I'm with you a hundred percent."

Now he looked peevish. "I just wish I could be sure you were really with me."

"Oh, honey, what do I need to do to convince you?"

"Stop flirting with him, for starters."

Stagey ignored that remark.

"Do you two need some privacy?" the cat woman sneered.

Stacey was the first to notice the far-off roar of the motor-cycles. She walked up to the sidewalk to make sure the Deputy Peavey was still there. He was, but the cycles were now within sight. She strained to try to recognize the cyclist who had shot the two addicts in Neola, but they all looked the same now. They were all wearing brown Conception Control uniforms, and they were all wearing masks. The first thing they did was surround Peavey's car. He promptly put on the siren and, speaking through a hand-held loudspeaker, ordered them to disperse. They trailed down the street in a long procession, but then executed an elaborate U-turn, daring the oncoming traffic to interrupt. They passed the patrol car coming back and turned into the lot where the table was set up. They circled the lot slowly while revving and backfiring their engines. The roar and the echoes made it impossible to talk, and the dust and smoke made it hard to see.

"Duck!" Stacey yelled. "They use chains. They'll drag you."

She kept her head almost flat to the table but kept her eyes open. Roland was frozen, his head on the table. Stacey put her hand on Grant's wrist to keep him from reaching into his shoulder holster. The cat lady watched with an expression of wrinkled resignation. The first cycle veered toward the table, then turned at the last second to circle around behind them. Another cycle turned towards the cat lady. She ducked away and grabbed Grant's free hand. More cycles feinted and steered around them, raising a horrific din.

All the motorcycles kept circling around the lot. But soon Peavey got out of his car and started filming the action, and the motorcyclists started trickling away, cutting dangerously close to his feet even as he filmed. Finally, the last one rumbled away. He took a quick glance at Stacey and friends, spoke into his radio, and sped off after them.

"Whew! Are all your rallies so exciting?" the cat lady spoke first.

"I was scared as shit," Grant breathed hard. "Thanks, Stacey. I could've shot somebody."

"She cares about you," Roland added, his voice dry like a challenge.

A memory clicked in Stacey's mind as she heard another low rumble. "I'm not sure it's over."

Another motorcycle appeared, made a wide turn onto the lot and stopped near the edge of the street. The Rider revved his engine and aimed his cycle straight for the table. Grant reached toward his holster. His gun went off with a deafening roar. The motorcycle bore down on the table. There was no time to run. The cyclist accelerated toward the table, raising his own gun and pointing it right at Stacey. He was ten feet away from Stacey when the arrow went through the middle of his chest.

*** ***

The dead cyclist's gun had not been fired. Grant's gun had been fired, but all the bullet did was graze his own hip and bury itself into the ground. In the confusion that followed, no one could say where the arrow came from. A few teenage boys, attracted by the noise, came and bounced around the lot, jabbering at full speed about what might have happened. Grant called 911. Stacey realized all the cops would be busy following the bulk of the Genesis Riders out of town. The fallen Rider was limp and covered with blood when they pulled him off the cycle. He wasn't breathing. Roland checked his neck for a pulse and there was none. It looked like the arrow had gone straight through his heart. Roland pulled off the Rider's helmet and mask. Dark hair, moustache, pale skin already turning blue. Stacey remembered that the guy who shot the addicts behind the record store in Neola had a moustache, but she couldn't be sure this was him.

The teenage boys helped them set up the chairs again, chattering all the while – then clammed up when the police arrived.

"These people are dangerous," Grant said. "We need to hire professional guards."

"Why are they doing this?" the cat lady asked no one in particular. "Why would these motorcycle ruffians care about a political event?"

"I think it's a deal," Grant answered. "We see it working out already in Neola County next door. The Certainty Party gets to set up an Old Testament theocracy in which women's only role is to serve men. The Genesis Riders terrorize everybody into obeying Ezekial, and in return they get money, control of the streets – and first crack at the women."

The police finally came and took a separate report from each witness. The deputies took Grant's gun and dug out the bullet from the ground before they left. The EMTs on the scene insisted that Grant be taken for evaluation at the hospital. He didn't want to go, but Stacey persuaded him by promising to go with him in the ambulance.

*** ***

"You didn't need to do that," Roland complained afterwards, the minute they were both back together in his apartment. "He wasn't seriously injured. You didn't need to ride along."

"What? I mean, he took a bullet for us, in a way."

"Ha! His own bullet."

"Okay. Okay. But he was trying to help, and protect me,

um, *us.*"

"Listen to yourself! You're still in love with him." He paced around his small living room, sat down on the davenport, turned his face down and away from her. His voice went weak and whiney. "You're still in love with him."

"Of course I'm not." She couldn't afford to be in love with Grant. She'd forced herself to face that on the plane ride home from Boston. That horrible plane ride when she decided that all men were too weak to rely on. Now Roland was proving her right.

She was beginning to think that a successful love life was more a matter of perseverance than anything else. Her mother's persistence had paid off, in the end. Her father had straightened himself out, and she was sure he would be coming back home eventually. And Stacey had come to love Roland in a different way. The handsome, articulate, confident, knowledgeable politician she knew at first had always seemed too good to be true. Now that his political support had been pulled out from under him by Golsch, and his mother had practically disowned him, he seemed like just an ordinary, decent man –who needed her support. A man who deserved her support. Even if he was getting a little peevish.

"I love you, and not him," she repeated.

"I want you to prove it." He turned away and walked toward his desk across the room.

"I haven't proven it already?" she said to his back.

He took a little box off his desk, then suddenly turned around and knelt in front of her. "Marry me."

"Of course. As soon as we can. Oh! Did Frieda …?"

"This has got nothing to do with Frieda," he cut her off. He opened the little box he was carrying and showed her a ring, a ring with a huge, radiant cut diamond, with channels of small diamonds on the band. "I want us to become officially engaged. I want you to wear this ring. Publicly."

"Roland, it's beautiful. And I love that you want me to wear it. But it doesn't seem right, while you're still married to somebody else."

"It is right. You're my soulmate, my salvation. And we're in this political fight together. We need to show everyone how together we are."

"They're already calling me a slut, a crack whore, a Jezebel, and who knows what else. Do we have to give them more ammunition? And what about Frieda? Wouldn't that be cruel to her?"

"You *will* wear this ring." He grabbed her hand and pushed it on her finger.

Chapter 33

First it was a trickle, then a flood. Terrified addicts abandoned the treatment centers in Neola County and raced to get into the already overcrowded centers in Cosgrove. It wasn't just the known, burnt-out addicts. Teenagers, housewives, office workers, farmhands, salesmen, warehousemen, truck drivers – and one minister – anybody who needed to buy drugs on a regular basis and was afraid their next buy could cost them their life. Audrey and Amy started a frantic campaign to convince more churches to house these addicts. Audrey came back in tears one evening.

"No luck, honey?" Don was a comforting presence now. He was affected by his wife's problems. He was not a zombie any more.

"No." She put her teary face into his chest. "No, Don. Just the opposite. I went to three new churches today. Every one of them offered to help. Everybody knows these addicts are going to be an awful lot of trouble, but everyone stepped up. I didn't expect that."

"Why not? You stepped up. You've done it for years, for me."

"Not really. I almost cracked, you know. When we mortgaged the house and then you blew all that money, too, I … I thought I couldn't keep on going."

"But you did."

"I did, didn't I? But I did it all *in anger*. These church people keep reminding me it can be done with love."

But there were a lot of people who didn't welcome the addicts, or the refugee women either. Reverend Ezekial excoriated Stacey, and Audrey and Amy, on *The Prophet* and his daily radio and weekly television show. "Cosgrove County has become a sinkhole of filth. Governor Adams ought to call in the KBI to clean it out. If she doesn't do something soon, I will talk to God. I will confer with God, and ask Him to send in his own troops."

Grant got over his embarrassment at his fiasco with the gun. He bought one for Ruth, too, and they went out target shooting together.

*** ***

Amy tracked her way up to Ruth's room upstairs. Ruth was sitting up straight on the edge of her bed, hands folded in her lap, her usual confident expression compromised by her tightly compressed lips. She seemed to be staring straight ahead into space.

"I saw you on TV," Amy started. "You were great."

"Oh." Ruth barely glanced over at her, but Amy saw the glaze of tears forming in her eyes. "I don't really know what's right or wrong. I just know what they are doing to my sister isn't right."

Amy sat down next to her without being invited. She unconsciously adopted Ruth's erect posture. Sitting like this on the bed, they were the same height.

"I didn't mean to ignore you since I moved in," Ruth offered. "I was raised not to trust anybody but my father."

"I'm used to being ignored. But you didn't even notice this?" She showed Ruth the brand on her forehead.

"Um, no. Oh, I'm sorry, Amy. Who did that to you?"

"The Genesis Riders. The religious police."

"I think your family is right. God couldn't have approved all these horrible things."

Amy didn't want to think about all those horrible things. "Do you miss being home?"

"Sometimes. I miss my mother, and my sister. But there's no point in going back." She stopped, then turned to Amy. "Maybe it's sinful to say, but when I think about what's happened, I miss my horse, Sugar Cookie, almost as much."

"You have a horse!"

"She's a bay mare. She's beautiful. I rode her almost every day."

"We used to have a mare named Foxie. Stacey rode her all the time. But she was gone by the time I was old enough. I never learned to ride."

Ruth's eyes lit up. "Maybe I can teach you." This was the first time Amy had seen her look so enthusiastic.

Amy knew instantly she wanted to do it. She explained there was a stable about twenty miles away, in south Cosgrove County. In safe country. Ruth lamented that she'd never been allowed to learn to drive a car.

"Not a problem," Amy explained. "I've been driving my mother's truck since I was fourteen."

Chapter 34

The new manager of television station WKTK aired another interview with Reverend Ezekial.

"It was already known," he said in response to a question about Stacey's opposition to the Make Our Motherhood Strong Act, "that she is engineering the kidnapping of unfortunate fallen women, keeping them from being re-baptized and reborn into God's grace. Now it's come out that she is an adulteress too. She should not be writing our laws. She should be on her knees, begging God's mercy."

"So, it is your belief that as an adulteress – and it has now been confirmed that Miss Davenport is living in sin with a married, current state delegate, Roland Asher – should not be allowed to make the laws on how our family lives are conducted?"

"Yes. She cannot be allowed to win this election. God and MOMS will prevail. The twisted, foul desires of that female Beelzebub will not defeat God and MOMS. MOMS will pass over the governor's veto. Because of Ms. Davenport's own history of filth and foulness, of sins against God and man, of betrayal and concupiscence and corruption, she will be crushed. This law will pass. With it, we will clean out her kind of filth and corruption. God Himself has revealed this to me.

"But then, in the greatness of His Almighty Being, God will demonstrate to Miss Davenport herself that even she is not beyond His transformative mercy. God will teach her obedience and repentance. She will be taught to pray to God for forgiveness, and to put herself in the hands of His holy messenger here on earth."

"I'm sure we all wish her well," the interviewer summed up on an upbeat note. "Thank you for your comments, Reverend Ezekial. I'm sure our listeners would like to continue to hear your opinions as this election period comes to a close. This station will make every effort to accommodate them."

"This is *news*?" Stacey and Roland were watching the show on the television in Roland's apartment. Roland looked like he was about to kick in the flatscreen. Stacey knew the risk of making him even angrier, but she couldn't resist. "This all comes from forcing me to wear your ring in public."

He turned to her, his face flushed. "No, it's not. People already knew we were living together. This is Robert Golsch. This is more payback for my not voting for the Professional Reform Act."

"I guess you're right." She wasn't really sure, but he had been showing more and more flashes of anger lately, and she didn't want to be the target this time.

"I know how to deal with him," Roland announced.

"This isn't the time for a big blow-up. The election is only two weeks away."

"I'm handling this!" Stacey had never seen him so angry before. He paced the room trying to calm himself down. "You don't think that broadcast hurt our chances? It could kill our campaign." He stopped pacing, and his breathing gradually slowed down. When he finally spoke, his voice was lower. "But I know how to handle Golsch."

*** ***

Roland found a little radio station that wasn't controlled by Golsch. It was outside his district, but he made sure his comments would be echoed throughout social media.

"By falling in love with Stacey Davenport, I have violated the civil laws of Kansas regarding marriage. But these are the laws of man, not the law of God. I love Stacey Davenport, and I think God has sent her to me to make me a better man." He paused for effect, being careful not to pause long enough to let the interviewer interrupt him.

"This attack on me, and on Stacey, has been orchestrated by Robert Golsch, the billionaire Kansas businessman who controls most of the broadcast stations in Kansas."

"Not this station." The interviewer was actually a DJ who had been asked by management to pepper in a few interviews of people with normal voices to counterbalance the hours his audience had to listen to his fake Texas drawl.

"I just want to add that this move by Robert deeply saddens me. My mother was a single mother who worked for him. We didn't have much money. But my whole life, Robert was very kind to my mother and paid a lot of attention to me. He was very, very attentive to me."

"Cut the crap. Is he your Daddy?"

Roland paused long enough for the implication of that question to sink in. "He was always giving me all kinds of presents, money. All the time. But sometimes, when my mother wasn't there …."

"What'd he do to you, son?"

"I won't say. I can't …. I don't want to talk any more about our personal relationship."

Within 24 hours, the new station manager of WKTK was fired and Bill Henderson was brought back. Reverend Ezekial would not get any more air time until after the election. Stacey would get an interview by herself.

"Golsch?" Stacey looked inquiringly at Roland the next time they met at their apartment. "What do you have on him?"

"A lot." Roland looked sad. "I didn't think it would come to this. It's really sad. The truth is, I was just making a threat. I would never reveal everything about him. I could never do that to him."

"I didn't think you had that kind of power over him."

"I told you I knew what I was doing."

*** ***

Roland's engagement ring was so ostentatious that any woman would notice it from twenty feet away. Stacey felt humiliated to be wearing a married man's engagement ring in public and took it off whenever it was safe to do so. She realized something was wrong. She should feel safe *with* Roland. But still, he loved her and he was on her side. He was under a lot of pressure. Grant kept showing up and doing a stand-up job for her campaign, but that wasn't helping Roland's mood at all.

As the days until the election wound down, it looked like she had regained the one point she had lost after Ezekial's adultery attack. The IT guy that Grant had brought with him from Liotech had set up probably the most sophisticated voting analysis system that had ever been used in a mere state legislative district. And for the past two weeks it had shown pretty much of a dead heat. The Liotech guy printed out every day the exact neighborhoods – specific addresses even – where they should go talk to people each day. There wasn't a targeted street that Stacey or a member of her family didn't canvass. And after running his printer in the machine shop where he was in hiding during the day, her father was delivering leaflets by night.

He wasn't the only one on the streets after dark. Powered by the promise of ruling the streets with violence, the ranks of the Genesis Riders were growing fast in neighboring Neola County. They had taken to cruising Cosgrove County in bands of seven or eight, and in too many groups for Randy and his deputies to keep track of. So far, they had scared a lot of women and forced a lot of zombies off the road, but nobody had been seriously hurt since the incident with the marko on Greyson Street in September. That incident had been the work of the local group of Riders, Randy explained. There had been only three of them, and one of them was dead. Neither of the other two had been seen since the night they attacked the kids in the field.

Chapter 35

"I think we got this election. Fifty-three percent for Stacey. One week until the vote. Hardly any undecided." The Liotech IT guy never went out on a limb. This meant she was going to win.

They were in her mother's living room, which was pretty much her unofficial campaign headquarters. Grant and Ruth and Audrey and Amy had come together there with Stacey for their last briefing on the polling and computer forecasting results.

Even Ruth, their square-shouldered, gun-toting stoic, broke into a smile. Stacey stole a glance at Grant. He had taught Ruth to use her natural intelligence and self-confidence to look at a wider and more complex world, and to learn from it. Stacey didn't think Ruth would ever go back voluntarily to live under her father's thumb. Grant had done that – and he had done that without seducing her. Ruth had actually kind of moved on from her crush on him and was talking to all kinds of other people now. If this whole campaign had taught just this one woman that she had the right to think for herself, it had been worth it. And Grant had done it. Stacey called him outside.

"You were wonderful with her. That's the only word to describe it. Wonderful."

"Aw, shucks," he said, but his voice was completely dry and deadpan.

"Don't make fun of me. I meant that from the heart. You were wonderful."

"Okay." He looked down. "It's nice to have a little piece of your heart." He tried to smile. "But it hurts. So can we just be friends – no, not even that – political allies, from now on?"

"Oh." She had thought they were at least friends. What he had done with the campaign and with Ruth was masterful.

But he didn't want to hear her effusive compliments now. She wondered what would have happened if she had answered any of his calls or texts on her way to the Boston airport or on the plane or during her first few days back in Kansas. All that was now a lifetime ago. Stacey looked at him, swallowed hard, and tried to shake off the disappointment she felt.

"I have to go." He walked past her and back into the house. "We did it!" she heard him say cheerfully to the group inside. "But let's not let our guard down now. There's some streets left we haven't canvassed a second time."

*** ***

Stacey was still alone on the porch, still upset, when Roland arrived.

"Everybody here? Why aren't you inside with them? What's wrong? The news is good, right?"

She couldn't tell him. And that's why he knew.

"I'll kill him!"

"He didn't do anything. No. Stop! What do you want? What more proof do you need that you're the one I love?"

He turned back, paused. "I've been thinking about that. I've come to a decision." His eyes suddenly narrowed. "I want you to marry me."

"Of course. As soon as we can legally …."

"It's being allowed right now in Neola County." He averted his eyes, but his features were set in stone.

"What!"

"Marry me now, Stacey! You'll be technically my second wife, but you'll always be the first to me."

"Have you lost your mind? *Second wife*! What do you think I – and my whole family, and *you* – have been fighting against all this time?"

"Along with Grant."

"Can't you accept that I'm choosing you instead of Grant? That I'll marry you as soon as we can legally do it? That I want you to be the father to my baby? Isn't that enough?"

*** ***

"Roland's making rules for me," she complained to her father the next night. "He has to approve all of my campaign talks, and he goes with me everywhere. And when he does, he makes it clear he's in control. It's embarrassing." She didn't mention his proposal that he be his second wife. She was hoping that ridiculous idea would just blow over.

"Oh, these politicians ...."

"And I can't talk to Grant unless there's a third person present in the room."

"Oh. He's jealous. That's a bad sign, Stacey."

"I guess."

"Has he ever hit you?"

"No. He has, you know, held my wrists." Even in the dim porchlight, she could see the look on his face. Her father was the only one she could talk to about this. She tried to explain about Roland. "He does love me. And everybody else he ever loved, Robert Golsch, his mother even, have turned against him – and all because he's stayed loyal to me, and my cause. I'm all he has. I can't bring myself to hurt him even more."

He turned and silently started to walk away.

"He needs me, Dad," she called after him. "He's doing right, and he really needs me. That's all he means."

Chapter 36

"I've heard from Robert Golsch."

Roland was whispering. They were in a pizza restaurant near his apartment and Stacey couldn't see any need to whisper.

"Roland, you need to tell me what happened between you and Golsch. I mean when you were a kid."

"Not so loud, please."

"All right. Let's start with: is he actually your father?"

"He acted like he was, until ...." He stopped cold, stared up at the chalkboard behind the counter showing the prices of the various pizzas. "My mother would never tell me who my father was."

"You said Golsch was nice, that he always acted like a father."

"It's true. He was always nice to me. But starting when I was like, thirteen ... I don't know what it was. It seemed strange. He would touch me – you know, rub my shoulders, massage my legs when I got cramps from football. He was always massaging me, touching me in different places. It was uncomfortable, but I didn't think it was that bad. I mean, I still don't exactly know how a father is supposed to act. When I was sixteen, my mother saw us doing it. She wouldn't let him come around after that. To me, it was like losing my father. And it felt like it was my fault he was banished."

"But you're still really close to him?"

"She let him come back when I was seventeen."

"Did ...?"

"No. No more massaging. And nobody ever talked about it."

"But you think he was, you know ...?"

"Now I do, of course. It's really so pathetic."

"Not pathetic, Roland. There was no way you could know what was going on. But it must be true, or he wouldn't have caved so easily and reinstated Bill Henderson as station manager of WKTK."

"You know something? I regret that. Not that the guy got his job back or that Ezekial was bumped from his prime-time pulpit on WKTK. What I regret is me doing it to Golsch. It was almost like blackmail."

"So he's retaliating now?"

"I think he's done with the retaliation now. We talked. It was almost like when I was seventeen. Just like when I was seventeen, when we both got amnesia about the bad stuff we did to each other."

Stacey was alarmed that he was talking to Golsch at all. It was ten days before the election. Stacey was still holding the tiny lead she had regained ever since Ezekial was banned from ranting against her on WKTK. The lead was three points, but the margin of error was four. Still, it seemed to be holding steady.

Roland explained what he had learned about the political details from Golsch. Golsch couldn't get his repeal of the minimum wage through without CP support. And the CP was still holding out for Golsch's help in overriding the governor's veto of The Make Our Motherhood Strong Act.

"Golsch is in a pickle. He can't get the repeal of the minimum wage from CP unless he gets all the independents to vote for MOMS. He needs every one now. And he's got all of them –

except me."

"And he's leaning on you hard, again?"

Roland nodded. Golsch was almost certainly his father. Not a perfect father, but maybe there was no such thing as a perfect father.

"Stacey, here's how hard he's leaning on me. He's offered me the Independent Party's nomination for governor if I help get MOMS through."

* * * * * *

Randy called her on the phone as she was driving back to Cosgrove, asking her to come in to the sheriff's office. He had something to tell her.

"The Genesis Riders are not only kidnapping women, they're terrorizing anybody who speaks out, whipping people in public. The Neola County sheriff is afraid of them." He reached for a manila folder on his desk. "But now I get something in the mail that makes me think it could get a whole lot worse."

He pulled out a letter from the file. The words were cut out of newspapers and magazines and pasted on, as in kidnappers' letters.

GENESIS RIDERS.
WE HAVE STOPPED YOU TWICE FROM MURDER. DO NOT SHOW YOUR FACE IN COSGROVE COUNTY OR SUFFER THE SAME FATE AS YOUR TWO SICK BROTHERS. KEEP OFF OUR WOMEN AND OUR ADDICTS.
THE EVOLUTIONARY GUARD

"Copies were sent to every newspaper in Kansas. No fingerprints, no forensic evidence. Mailed from Kansas City. But you see what I'm saying. This violence could get much worse."

✳✳ ✳✳

Ruth and Grant were openly carrying nine-millimeter pistols in holsters everywhere they went. They claimed they knew how to use them now. Ruth had taken over the organization of the Cosgrove Baptist Church shelter on the town square. Audrey was relieved to be able to work full time on the campaign. Ruth convinced three of the women to buy guns and practice with her. They heard the rumble of motorcycles at least once a night. So far, they had just closed the doors and windows and turned out all the lights. So far, the Riders would simply roar up and down the street in front of the shelter until they got bored or the sheriff chased them off.

Stacey followed Roland's instructions and made sure she was never alone in a room with Grant. She actually liked this arrangement. She couldn't stand the icy civility Grant used toward her now. His coldness didn't seem fair.

But she had bigger things to worry about. She had gotten over her morning sickness weeks ago, and she had never been slowed down in the least by her pregnancy, but now she thought she could feel her little girl growing inside her. A kind of slow happiness came over her, and she had to fight constantly to keep up her edge. She couldn't imagine how her mother had managed to support and raise the three of them by herself.

Her pregnancy was a safe topic to talk about with Roland. He was overjoyed that it was a girl, a "new little Stacey," as he called her. They both ignored the fact that Grant was the biological father. But that issue would be hard to avoid in the long run. She wished she could talk to Grant just as a friend, but apparently neither man wanted her to do that.

Then Grant raised the baby issue directly with Roland, and Roland erupted. He demanded that Grant be fired from the campaign.

"He's a volunteer."

"He's in your campaign headquarters every day. When he's not there, he's in your mother's house. He's after you, and you can't even see it."

"Look, Roland, he won't even talk to me."

"And you're hurt by that. Don't try to deny it."

She fired Grant. She made Ruth tell him. She still needed the Liotech computer guy and was relieved when Grant did not pull him off the campaign. But Roland found out about that.

"Get that Liotech nerd out, too," he commanded, just as she arrived at his apartment.

"Come on, Roland. We need him. And it's only five more days."

"He's a gift from Grant. You're still accepting gifts from Grant." He stepped forward, crowding her.

She backed away, put down her things, then came up to him and put her hands gently on his chest. "You know I do everything I can to make you happy." She started to rub her hands over him very softly, trying to remind him wordlessly of their physical connection. But this just added another dimension to his jealousy. He brushed her hands away.

"I can't count on you! I can't count on you is the problem. I need you, Stacey, but you're always trying to sneak away."

"That's not true."

He was breathing hard. He was angry, and aroused. She'd seen him in this state before. She hated to use sex as an escape hatch, but sometimes it worked.

But he pushed her away again. "No! I need to *have* you, Stacey. All of you. Now. Here's what we're going to do. We're going to get married, in Neola County, tonight."

Without a word, she turned to pick up her things and go. Her knees were shaking. She'd been making excuses for him for weeks. She'd denied to herself that she was going along with his controlling behavior. She'd hoped that if she placated him a little, he would get better. She'd always reminded herself that he didn't have much of a family and it was natural for him to put a lot of weight on their relationship. But things had gotten worse. Now he wanted to humiliate her in front of the whole world. Controlling and humiliating her seemed to be a basic need of his. She reached the door and had her hand on the doorknob.

"If you walk out." The voice behind her was cold. "If you walk out, I'll sign off on the Make Our Motherhood Strong Act tonight."

She jerked herself around. "You wouldn't!" But after his attitude the last few days, she wasn't so sure.

Now his voice was whiney. "It's all because I love you, Stacey. I need you so much."

"You love me so much you'd send forty thousand women into concubinage?"

"I feel sorry for them. I do. But unless you marry me voluntarily, the Make Our Motherhood Strong Act is the only way I will ever get you. If MOMS passes, you'll be assigned to Reverend Ezekial, and I can make a deal with him for you. If that's the only way I can get you, I will."

He stared at her. He'd thought all this out. She hadn't. Even if she won the election, she wouldn't take office for another twenty days. If he signed on to MOMS now, it would become law now. She walked past him and went out to the balcony and leaned onto the rail, the same rail where she'd first felt the power of his jealousy weeks ago. Since the moment he took her there weeks ago, her love for him had gradually changed, from admiration to rationalization to accommodation. Now it was changing to fear. He might tell himself that he was a good guy, but in his soul he was really one of *them*.

He walked out onto the balcony after her.

"Don't touch me – or I swear I'll jump," she shouted. "I'd die rather than be your concubine. And I'm not afraid of dying."

He stared at her. She could tell he believed her. He was

obviously shaken by the thought of losing her. But then a little smile crept slowly onto his face.

"Stacey, if you jump, I'll sign onto MOMS anyway."

A shiver of revulsion ran through her. This man would make thousands of women pay with their freedom if he didn't get what he wanted. And the only thing he wanted was her.

"You would be so cruel?" she managed.

"You don't know how much I need you – a hundred million times more than all those other women put together."

Even as she tried to think this through, she felt sick, because she already knew the answer. There was no other honorable choice. The only way to save Amy and thousands of other women in Kansas from becoming concubines was to become one herself.

She knew from her study of history that many people had sacrificed themselves so that others might live free. She had never imagined herself as this kind of savior.

But there it was.

Chapter 37

When a man sells his daughter as a slave, she will not be freed at the end of six years as the men are. If she does not please the man who bought her, he may allow her to be bought back again. – Exodus 21: 7-8.

She was still holding onto a three-percent lead the day before the election. Roland had let her keep the Liotech IT guy, and they identified and canvassed the last 163 undecided voters that afternoon. Roland went with her and made sure she wore her engagement ring all the time. Nevertheless, they were a good-looking, outgoing couple, and she thought they might have convinced a few voters to go her way. Nobody asked about the ring.

Audrey was avoiding her. It might have been because of that shameful ring, but more likely it was because Stacey had let her believe all these years that it was Don who had stolen her paychecks. There was no way to calculate the damage done between her mother and father by that lie. There was no way to repair it now. And things would only get worse when her mother found out Stacey was soon to become Roland's concubine.

Roland had agreed they wouldn't get married until late afternoon on election day. News wouldn't leak out until it was too late to affect the election results. They would leave for Neola at 4:30 p.m. that day. Stacey wasn't planning to tell anyone until then. Roland promised that after they were married, he would still let her go to Topeka and take her seat in the legislature. This gave her some hope that he was still basically a good guy, even if he was obsessed with her.

Family, friends and shelter women were scattered to work

the polls on election morning. It seemed that Grant was still trying to help from afar. At least, Liotech paid for exit polling, which showed by 3:00 p.m. that Stacey might have a one percent lead. She wished she could stay and work the polls until they closed, but they had to leave by 4:30 for the wedding. She left a separate written note for each member of her family, and for Corinne and Ruth. She begged them not to be angry and asked them to understand that she was making this sacrifice for all the other women in Kansas. She planned to text them from Neola with the details of the wedding when it would be too late for them to do anything about it.

She told her father the night before that she had consented to be Roland's second wife. He was crushed. "Just when things were going great. You're going to win. Your mother is softening up on letting me come home."

"I have to do it."

"Believe me, Stacey. I know what it's like to be treated as a subhuman. It's no fun." He took his hoodie off and pushed his thick hair back all the way and she saw in the porchlight, clearly for the first time, the mark branded into his forehead.

"Oh!" She whimpered at the sight of it. But she had to say her piece. "He's really okay. If he could legally divorce Frieda right now, he would. This is the only way he can have me. He'll treat me well, I'm sure."

"I can smuggle you out of Kansas. We'll be in a blue state by tomorrow."

"If I do that, the Make Our Motherhood Strong Act will be law within 24 hours. All the other women will be rounded up. Including Ruth and Amy."

She said goodbye. She knew she'd have no absolute right to see him again. She wished she'd paid more attention, recently, to all the ways he seemed to have invented to get around the rules.

Roland was suspicious when she left the polling place a

few minutes early to stop at her mother's house on the way to Neola. "Don't be ridiculous. You have me in your complete control. I just want to take a shower." Really, she just wanted to talk to somebody there. Anybody.

Kendrick was home, with Corinne, making out on the davenport in the living room. Kendrick's face went red, but Corinne looked up brightly. "We're going to win, I'm sure."

She sat down opposite them. "Corinne, I can't tell you how much it has meant ... all that you've done to help. To help Kendrick, and all of us. Kendrick, you came through, you learned who your friends are. You've grown. I really believe in you guys. And I always will. Remember that."

She wanted to tell them about the wedding, but she couldn't. They didn't say anything. Then she figured out why. They were probably just waiting for her to go so they could continue making out. She guessed she had missed that stage of teenage life by spending her time worshipping the needle in her arm. She left them alone. She didn't take a shower. Roland was making all the arrangements anyway, including her dress. She waited outside for him to pick her up.

Amy walked up. "Out of leaflets," she explained. "I've been talking to everybody. You're going to win."

"I love you, Amy."

"Well, yeah."

Stacey told her what she was doing, and why. Amy cried. But Stacey explained that there was no other way. No other way to save all the women, including Amy herself. She begged Amy to keep in contact with her father, and to stay off the streets. Roland arrived a little later. Stacey jumped in his car and waved goodbye to her little sister.

"How is this going to work?" she asked him. "Won't the courthouse be closed by the time we get there?"

"Church wedding."

"Oh, come on. You're kidding."

"Reverend Ezekial is going to marry us."

*** ***

They reached Ezekial's gigantic church complex. The ceremony for second wives could normally be held only in a side chapel, but Ezekial had made an exception for her. Stacey was forced to wear an outfit designed by Ezekial. It was a long, pleated, beige jumper that fell halfway between her knees and her ankles over a white blouse with a Peter Pan collar. The shoes were black leather oxfords. The tiny veil was beige also. She was not allowed to talk to Roland once they entered the church complex, so there was nobody to complain to.

"This is the way you will show yourself at the altar," the woman who dressed her said. The woman herself was wearing a white collar over a loose brown dress that went down to her ankles. "Once you're married, you'll wear standard second wife's garb every day. If your husband allows, you'll be able to wear a different outfit on the Sabbath."

"Do you like dressing this way?"

"*Women must adorn themselves in modest apparel, with shamefacedness and sobriety; not with braided hair, or gold, or pearls, or costly array.* That's what the Bible says."

"Oh. Okay. Um, are you someone's second wife?" Stacey asked.

"Third."

"Are you happy being a third wife?"

"God is pleased with my service."

"Who's your husband?"

"I can't tell his name without permission."

She dreaded appearing in the nave of the church, and the dread got worse when she heard organ music from the choir loft. They had both insisted that the Genesis Riders not be allowed inside, but a large crowd of jeering Riders was just outside the building, starting and revving their engines from time to time in violation of the minister's orders. She could also hear a lot of people inside the church, and she now saw that Reverend Ezekial had designed this ceremony to be her ultimate humiliation. But why was Roland going along with it? She texted him and asked him why.

> *Because he has all the power in this county. Don't worry. We'll get this over with.*

> *There must be twenty photographers here. I'm not sure I can do this.*

> *You'll have to say a lot of things at the altar. Forget what they make you say. You are my soul mate. Once we're married, Frieda is going to be the second wife.*

> *She'll be the concubine?*

> *I promise you she'll have clean quarters.*

She didn't try to look happy in the hundreds of photographs that were taken as she walked down the aisle, but she didn't want to look defeated either. She settled on a competent, let's-get-this-over-with look. Roland was smiling like a twenty-year-old boy getting ready to marry his teenage dream girl. She forced herself to look up and meet Ezekial's gaze. Ezekial smirked. "This is more than I ever hoped for, Stacey – to see you buried alive."

She should have guessed that Frieda would be there. Still, he was shocked to see her former friend walk slowly out of the sacristy a moment after Ezekial. Frieda then took up a position standing on the other side of Roland. It seemed like Ezekial had pulled out all the stops to make Stacey as miserable as possible.

Stacey had already betrayed her former friend in private;

now she had to do it right in front of her, and in public. She didn't know who was more humiliated. Frieda was wearing what looked like her original white wedding dress, which still fit her perfectly. Her face was pale and her mouth was set in a grim line. She was holding Roland's left hand in a tight grip. Stacey forced herself to look into her eyes. Frieda stared back, a streak of hatred forcing its way through a blank look of despair.

Reverend Ezekial had obviously planned which of the two of them he would humiliate the most. He made her kneel down in front of Frieda.

"Repeat after me. *I am honored to recognize you, Frieda, as the lawful first wife of Roland.*"

Stacey repeated.

"*I promise to obey you in all matters without delay, and without question.*"

Stacey repeated.

"*I will never offend you in any way.*"

Stacey thought it was a little too late for that, but she repeated it. Frieda shook her head almost imperceptibly, her eyes stony.

"*From this day forward, I will be be known as Zilpah, after the handmaiden to Jacob's wife, Rachel. As Rachel gave Zilpah to Jacob as his concubine, so I rejoice that Frieda permits me to serve both her and Roland.*"

Stacey stumbled and stopped. Ezekial made her start again and complete the vow, louder, so her voice could be heard clearly through the multiple microphones clipped to the lectern nearby.

"And to you, Master Roland Asher, let me remind you of the words of God. *If a man marries another woman, he must not deprive the first one of her food, clothing and marital rights.* Exodus 21:10." Then Reverend Ezekial turned so he was facing both Stacey and Frieda. "And to both of the wives, I remind you of the words of the New Testament: *A woman should learn in quietness and full submission. I do not permit a woman to teach or to have authority over a man; she must be silent. 1 Timothy 2: 11-12."*

She hated herself for going through with this. She hated herself even more for trying to take Roland from Frieda in the first place. And she hated Frieda, too, for coming and participating in this ceremony. Was she so stupid she believed in all this crap? Couldn't she see they were both victims here, victims of Ezekial's and Roland's twisted egos? Then she was surprised when Frieda suddenly reached out and gently touched her shoulder. That obviously wasn't part of the plan. Ezekial abruptly ended this part of the ceremony. Stacey found herself hoping they'd be allowed to talk to each other during the marriage. Ezekial shuffled her back to the middle of the altar.

She turned and faced the congregation, which mostly consisted of reporters and a few identically dressed women who Stacey guessed were second wives. Then she saw Kendrick and Corrine. Why were they here? Neither of them was old enough to drive, and Neola County was a dangerous place for any teenage girl. But she was glad they were there, if only to bear witness to her shame. Teenagers were used to shame, she knew.

The beginning was a standard protestant ceremony, except Reverend Ezekial stretched out the word "God" each time, as if he owned the name. Roland took her hand and held it right from the beginning. She knew he thought he loved her, but she also knew he got some kind of satisfaction out of seeing her humble herself. It could have been Ezekial who arranged for all this news coverage, but she suspected Roland had done it himself. The power he had over her now had gone to his head. Roland was not at all the man she had thought he was. Life with him was going to be worse than she'd imagined. She tried to numb herself to everything that was going on. She blanked out whatever Ezekial was saying.

"Yes, I object." A halting, cracking teenage male voice

sang out from the congregation. Ezekial's mouth dropped, and the reporters turned around. It was Kendrick. Ezekial, she realized, had just asked the standard question of whether anyone objected to this couple coming together. Kendrick had objected. Now he stood up.

"He hits her. I've seen it." Kendrick's face got redder. His voice cracked again. "This is wrong. Don't do it, Stacey."

Roland looked enraged. Stacey had no idea what color her own face was. *Don't do this, Kendrick.* But her little brother had such faith in her she owed him an explanation. She stepped forward toward the congregation.

"Kendrick is my little brother. He sees only the good in me. But Kendrick, I'm not perfect. I've done a lot of bad things. Roland isn't perfect either, but he needs me. I'm here to willingly give myself to him.

"And after today, MOMS will be defeated, and kidnapping and rape will still be illegal in Kansas. The women in the shelters in Cosgrove will be free to return home. Our sister Amy will not be assigned to be some married man's concubine.

"I'm the last one, the last second wife. And at least this wedding is a happy one."

Roland grabbed her arm, leaned in toward her. "Good girl. But I told you, *Frieda* is going to be the second wife."

What did he really mean by that? She was definitely his second wife according to God's law as interpreted by Ezekial and the Genesis Riders in Neola County. Could he change that?

He seemed to think he could change anything. He had made her wear that ring showing she was engaged to him, a married man, in public. He had finished her sentences for her in public speeches. He had made her fire Grant. He could change his promise that she would be the first wife, too. A first wife could go out and visit and talk to whoever she wanted. But for how long would he be able to stand seeing her talking to anyone else but him? How long would it be until she would be the one confined to the "clean quarters?"

She had been an addict long enough to know you could find drugs anywhere, under any conditions. Would she end up seeking oblivion that way?

She caught a sudden glimpse of her father sitting alone up in the choir. She could even see the mark on his forehead. As soon as their eyes met, he ducked back. As a marked addict, he wasn't supposed to be in any public gathering, but Roland had gotten him a special pass for today. It was legal for him to be here. But he had said he wasn't coming.

Now something she had seen that morning suddenly made sense. Early that morning, she had searched all the saddlebags on his motorcycle looking for an ankle bracelet. She was going to wear it to the wedding as a sign of protest. Even if no one else could see it under her dress, she would know it was there. But she hadn't been able to find one.

What she did find made her catch her breath. Now, seeing her father hiding up there in the choir, watching over her, she finally understood. She understood now who shot the Rider who was trying to chain-whip Corinne at the kids' group meeting in the field. She knew where that arrow she had found in the field that night had come from. She knew who had shot that Genesis Rider in Orwell without a sound. It was him. Her father was the Evolutionary Guard.

Chapter 38

"Do you, of the current name of Stacey Davenport, soon to be renamed Zilpah, take this man to be your lawfully wedded husband?"

"No." She glanced up at the choir. She had guessed right. She saw her father's eyes. She shook her head no.

She stepped in front of Roland and embraced him, but suddenly pushed him roughly away from the lectern. "We have to get out of here. Your life is in danger."

"Don't give me that shit. Don't think you can say no." Roland grabbed her tightly. "I can take you right here and now. I don't need your agreement."

"Don't push your luck. I just saved your life."

With a wooden cracking sound, the arrow shattered the lectern behind them. Bradbury, Ezekial's personal assistant, grabbed him and dragged him out a side door. Stacey kept pushing Roland to the side until he was out of the line of sight from the choir, then wrenched herself free, turned back and ran across the altar and back up through the aisle outside.

Outside, she had to pick her way through the crowd of catcalling Genesis Riders. Then the tone changed as Roland appeared at the church door, looking confused. Suddenly Corinne appeared in front of Stacey and threw a handful of rice in her face. "Listen!" She pulled Stacey's head down to her and pretended to kiss her on the cheek. "Your father's left one of his magic motorcycles for you behind that giant tree next to the parking lot. Run for it."

She looked back and saw Roland just a few steps behind. He was walking at a controlled but brisk pace, as if there were no danger. She ran to him and embraced him again. "It's my father. He's the Evolutionary Guard. We have to get out of here fast." She pushed him toward the parking lot. "Stay close to me or he might shoot again."

The crowd didn't seem to realize there was any danger. The women in their second-wife garb stood toward the back, hoping to get a glimpse of their new compatriot on her way out. The rest of the crowd were Genesis Riders, and they were either leering their congratulations at the new couple or just plain mocking Stacey. Stacey and Roland rushed through the crowd, holding hands, heads lowered. When they reached the parking lot, they saw the matrimonial limousine pulling out onto the street. Bradbury was at the wheel. Reverend Ezekial had commandeered the only nearby car.

"Over here. My Dad left a motorcycle."

"Never walk away from me again!" Roland stepped forward and slapped her across the face.

"Oh." She put her hands to her face and tried to push back the tears from coming out. She had saved his life, but he still couldn't see the big picture. His world was getting smaller and smaller. His jealousy was getting worse and worse. He was deranged, and he was dangerous. She tried to back away from him, but he grabbed her with one hand and raised his fist to hit her again.

She twisted away and stumbled back across the empty parking lot. She regained her balance, but he came after her. She took a panicked step back. Something moved inside her. She took two, three steps back. Four steps. Five.

The arrow hit Roland in the chest and he crumpled to the asphalt. She froze, then forced herself to stumble forward and kneel beside him. His blood was spurting out fast. He was dead in thirty seconds – without a word or a gesture or a hint of recognition, his eyes open in a dead man's stare. The crowd was far back, hidden from the parking lot by the trees, and hadn't seen it happen. She got up and left in a panic. Roland's blood was still smeared on her hands and face and all over her second-wife's jumper. She found the motorcycle her father

213

had left for her. She ripped her dress getting on, and it flew out behind her like wings as she sped away like a bat out of hell.

* * * * * *

Frieda came down the church steps holding her own train bunched in her arms. The Genesis Riders didn't know what to make of a first wife, especially one wearing a bridal gown and crying. Word got around that a young teenager had objected to the wedding and that it hadn't gone through. Kendrick was soon chest bumped to the ground. A Rider grabbed Corinne by the hair and started dragging her off. Kendrick stood up, screaming, until one of the other Riders backhanded him across the face and knocked him to the ground again. The Riders were all laughing now, the sudden violence relieving the tension of living in a world they didn't understand.

"Stop it!" Frieda screamed from her perch on the church steps. "Stop it! Stop it!" It wasn't as if the Riders were shocked by hearing a woman screaming at them. For many of them it was normal background noise to their lives. But Frieda's commanding voice and posture, together with the gown gathered up well above her knees, made them pause. "Leave those children alone."

Corinne's would-be abductor let go of her hair. The rest of them stepped back so Kendrick could get back on his feet. The teenagers rushed to each other and quickly filtered their way out of the crowd. They ran through the trees and across the parking lot toward the street where they'd parked Audrey's old truck. But then they stopped dead. Corinne screamed and buried her face in Kendrick's chest.

"Help!" Kendrick shouted back to the crowd. "Need help here." Kendrick sounded like he wasn't sure these were the people he should ask for any kind of help, but he kept yelling. "It's Roland! He's messed up! Somebody call an ambulance."

The couple ran off hand-in-hand to the truck, and Kendrick quickly started the engine. They could hear men yelling, women screaming, motorcycles revving, and screeching tires behind them. Then there was the siren of an approaching ambulance.

Chapter 39

She was riding probably the only motorcycle in Kansas quiet enough make a cell call from.

"Mom?"

"Hold it, Stacey. I'm putting the IT guy on!"

"Stacey, we won!"

"Put my Mom back on."

"Oh, honey. You won! You don't need him now. You can vote against it."

"Listen. The Genesis Riders are coming to Cosgrove. They are after me, and they're super pissed. Call Randy. He's got to protect the shelters. Get Grant to protect your house, get Ruth. And call Kendrick. Tell him and Corinne to stay away from the house."

She stayed off the phone then and concentrated on driving on the tiny back roads and dirt roads where the Riders wouldn't find her. She drove as fast as she dared, but it was more than 40 minutes later before she came within a half mile of the house. Even from there she could tell it was burning. Up close, the downstairs windows were broken and blazing and the upstairs had disappeared into a huge cloud of white smoke. The Cosgrove Volunteer Fire Department had just arrived. She saw them drag something heavy in a tarp away from the house.

"Who is that? Why are you being so rough?" She dropped her cycle and ran toward the two guys pulling the tarp. One was a young kid not much older than Kendrick and the other one she recognized as John, the owner of the downtown pizza place. The older one wouldn't meet her eyes. The young fireman looked up, staring.

"Ma'am, you're injured."

"No, I'm fine."

"You're covered in blood. You could be in shock. Let me

get the EMTs here."

"I'm fine! I'm fine!" she insisted. "Just tell me. Who is in the tarp?"

"It's a dog. He's dead. He wasn't burned up. He was shot."

She watched them dump the dog at the edge of the lawn. The young fireman ran toward the waiting ambulance. The other firefighters were frantically trying to put out the blaze. She heard shots coming from the direction of downtown Cosgrove. Stacey couldn't afford to waste time being examined by the EMTs. And this was not the time to grieve for Shelbie.

*** ***

On their way back from Neola, Kendrick and Corinne got a call from Grant. He told them the Riders were circling, swinging chains, harassing them as they ran toward the shelter. The Riders had shot Shelbie.

"Stay away. Don't come into town." Grant was breathing heavily, as if he were running hard. "Okay. Okay. Your mother and Ruth and Amy and I are safe in the shelter now."

"Where's Stacey?"

"We haven't seen her since she left for the wedding in Neola."

"What should we do?"

"Go to Corinne's house. Don't come here. They're shooting guns in the air."

"I thought you had a gun, Grant."

"Yeah, well, they took it away."

Kendrick turned to Corinne the minute he hung up. "Has your father got any guns?"

When Kendrick and Corinne arrived at the shelter, a sheriff's car was parked in the bright pool of light in front of the shelter while the Genesis Riders were circling the empty park in front of that church building, stirring up a choking cloud of dust.

The Riders didn't seem to have any clear plan, and they didn't have any obvious leader. Deputy John Peavey was using his bullhorn, ordering them to disperse, but they just swerved closer to the patrol car. They were screaming for Stacey to come out. Peavey told them through PA speakers that Stacey wasn't there, but they ignored him and circled even closer. Kendrick pulled up a hundred yards away, cut the truck's motor, and watched.

The Riders skimmed closer and closer to the deputy's car until one of their cycles scraped it. Flashing his lights and sounding his siren, the deputy chased the rider, jumping the curb and following him into the park, stirring up even more dust. The rest of the Riders erupted in jeers and laughter. Then they headed to the door of the shelter. A muscular Rider, a little gone to fat, his shaved head shining in the shelter's bright security lights, skidded to a stop right in front of the door. He kick-standed his cycle and jumped off, leaving the motor running. He moved to the rack on the back. There was a red plastic gas can strapped on. The muscles in his arms visibly shook as he hurriedly tried to loosen the straps. Then he grabbed the can and rushed toward the massive wooden door. Some of the other Riders pulled to a stop to watch, while others kept circling, keeping John Peavey busy chasing them. Kendrick, watching, started the truck's engine.

One side of the giant oaken door suddenly swung open. Ruth stepped out, standing tall and straight and with a pistol in her hand. She raised it and pointed it right at the gas can guy's chest. He screamed at her not to shoot. He ran back toward his cycle, dropping the can. She stepped forward and kicked the can toward him. The circling riders swerved away. The gas can man's motor stalled and the can lodged against the back wheel. Just as he got it started again, she took careful aim and shot the can. The back of the motorcycle exploded into flame just as he got it going, and he sped up, going straight down the street like a comet with a tail of fire. The remaining riders took off, but in a few minutes they circled back, one of them swinging a chain, Deputy Peavey's car right behind.

*** ***

Stacey hadn't realized how much dried blood was in her hair until she tried to pull her mask on over it. She was pretty sure the gunshots were coming from the shelter. She knew her family and friends would run there.

When she heard the Riders on the streets near the shelter, she rolled her white Peter Pan collar inward. As she reached the town square, two Riders rode right past her without noticing. She edged around the square towards the shelter, now unafraid, as numerous Riders passed by without seeing her. When she came within sight of the bright circle of light in front of the shelter door, she saw a Rider poised on his cycle, fifty feet away, swinging a chain. She couldn't see who was his intended victim until she squinted past the glare into the softer circle of light. There, she saw Ruth, backed against the dark wooden door. She had a pistol in her hand pointed directly at the Rider. The Rider was moving very slowly forward.

The door suddenly opened and another woman came out. She backed herself against the door across from Ruth. Stacey could see she was holding a rifle, which she quickly brought up to draw a bead on the Rider. And Stacey could see it was Amy.

Stacey drove into the center of the circle of light.

"No, Amy! Don't do this!"

Amy didn't even turn her head. "Shut up. I can at least fight. You're not the only one."

Stacey heard the whir of the chain not six inches from her head. She threw herself to the ground. Peavey's cruiser pulled into the circle, almost running her over. Stacey jumped up and pulled on the driver's side door. Peavey looked terrified. She yanked the door open, then pulled off her mask so he could see her face. Peavey didn't look any less terrified.

"I'm Stacey Davenport. Give me your bullhorn."

She climbed on top of his cruiser. The chain guy melted into the crowd in the darkness.

"Go home. Nobody's been hurt. You haven't committed any crimes, yet."

"Give us the women." Stacey didn't recognize the voice, and she couldn't see the speaker in the darkness.

"I know Ezekial gives you five hundred bucks for each woman. Did you know he sells them for ten thousand?"

There was thirty seconds of silence. Then: "We get to fuck them first."

"We have three women in here who have brothers in the Genesis Riders. Who wants to sell his own sister?"

Chapter 40

"First, my heart goes out to Roland Asher, to his parents, to his friends, and to all those in the Independent movement which he led. Nobody relied on his insight, sagacity and courage more than I did. His death is a great loss for our political system, our state, and our country. And I know it's a much greater loss for his family and friends. To all of you, my deepest condolences."

She had barely had time to wash his dried blood out of her matted hair. She'd barely had time to think of him at all before giving her victory speech. But as she spoke these words of praise for him, she realized they were true. He had been on his way to becoming a great man. Until he met her. She turned away to brush away the tears that came to her eyes. But she had to go on.

"I want to thank everybody who helped in our campaign – our *successful* campaign!" The expected cheers rose from the small crowd of family, campaign workers and women residents gathered at the shelter. "But first, I want to express our gratitude to Sheriff Randy Crenshaw. Randy resolved a standoff right outside this building earlier tonight that was about to degenerate into a violent battle, a potentially deadly battle that could have triggered a civil war throughout the whole state of Kansas. Randy stepped in, unarmed, between two armed and angry groups, and defused the situation, using only the power of his moral authority. Randy, that moral authority is true, and deep. The citizens of Kansas will be forever in your debt."

Randy was standing at the back of the shelter. He smiled at her accolade and winked when she looked his way. They both knew she was exaggerating. They both knew it was Stacey who had taken the starch out of the Genesis Riders. They hadn't been ready for a Valkyrie soaked in blood to be challenging them from the top of a police car. They were shocked when she told them Ezekial was ripping them off. They were ashamed to think they might be enslaving their own sisters. By the time Randy sped into the square and got out of his cruiser, the Riders had been reduced to a demoralized mob. It also didn't hurt that Randy told them that Governor Adams, upon hearing of Stacey's election victory, had finally gotten the courage to authorize the state police to come in and protect the shelter.

Stacey knew this speech was probably broadcast all over Kansas. She would not give up the chance to make her point. "As a legislator, I will do everything in my power to help Governor Adams resist Reverend Ezekial's plans to subjugate women. I want to convince the people of Kansas that he does not speak to God any more than you or I do. He is a kidnapper, a man who trades young women like other men trade old cars. He is, in a word, a false prophet.

"And I have a word for Robert Golsch. I know that you do not share Reverend Ezekial's religious beliefs. Yet you fund the election of every member of the Certainty Party, and you help them enact their most barbaric, pre-Christian beliefs into law. In return, they enact any economic legislation you want. Breaking up this hypocritical, unholy alliance will be one of my top priorities. I will expose you. I will take you on."

The crowd applauded and cheered, though most of them did not know what she was talking about. The link between Golsch and the Certainty Party was known only to the closest observers of the political scene in Topeka. Very few in the media had shown the courage to try to expose this alliance.

"But I also want to speak to everyone about a deep need that we all have. We all crave certainty. We crave the feeling that everything we do is in accordance with God's will. We need that feeling so badly we do crazy things. We worship little pieces of bread, we flog ourselves in public, we wear special underwear. The only good thing about being a heroin abuser was I knew exactly what I wanted every minute of the day. No, I'm not comparing heroin addiction to religion. I'm saying that certainty itself is a kind of drug. Absolute certainty can keep you from new experiences, new people, unexpected joys. It can lead you down violent and unholy paths. Absolute certainty is something only God has a right to. Nobody on this earth should ever claim it."

*** ***

It was after midnight. Her unofficial campaign headquarters in Audrey's house was a smoldering ruin. Corinne's mother had invited them all over to rest while they figured out what to do next. Grant was there. His tone was suddenly humble. He was acting like her friend again. The danger they'd all been through that night had obviously mellowed him out, at least for the time being.

"I refused to marry Roland, in the end," she told him now.

He found something to say. "To be his second wife. We all read the notes you left us. But I know you, Stacey. I didn't want to believe you would ever really agree to that. I guess I was right."

"I just hope my daughter won't have to grow up in all this chaos."

Stacey decided not to tell him the whole story.

*** ***

Randy was sitting on Corinne's mother's sofa, his eyes drooping from exhaustion. Stacey sat down next to him. "I meant every word I said about you tonight. Ruth and Amy were ready to shoot. Hendrick and Corinne had guns, too. One wrong move, and all hell would have broken loose."

"Yeah. That shows you what can happen when law enforcement breaks down."

"It's more than a law enforcement problem, Randy. It's a *religious* problem. People have got to learn that God doesn't speak through just one person."

"You know, I think most everybody really knows that, Stacey."

"So if people know God is not speaking through Ezekial, why are half the people in this state following him like robots?"

Randy sighed. "I've been a sheriff a long time. I've seen how it goes. A lot of people will sign on to almost anything if there's something in it for them. A lot of the time it's money."

"But it's not money, Uncle Randy. Ezekial is constantly sucking money out of his followers. He's not giving them a dime. He's costing them money."

"There's something more powerful than money, honey. Call it pride. The idea that your kind is better than some other kind. You tell one group they're better, closer to God than the other – almost everybody will be a sucker for that one."

*** ***

Amy had been avoiding her ever since the showdown at the shelter. Stacey cornered her in the kitchen. "That made me sick, Amy, to see you pointing that gun." Amy said nothing, just gave her a sour look in response. Stacey sensed there was some kind of tension between the two of them, a new tension she didn't quite understand. "Don't you realize, Amy, once you point a gun like that, it gives anybody else the right to shoot you."

"Don't you realize, Stacey, they're still taking women at gunpoint? That Ruth's sister, Renee, is still a captive, right now? I swear I'm going to do something about it, Stacey. I'm not like you."

"Nobody has ever said you were like me," Stacey laughed.

"Right. They never said I was like you. They said not as

good as you."

"Nobody ever said that!" People turned to look. Stacey begged Amy with her eyes to move into a corner of the room where they could not be overheard.

"Not in so many words." Amy's delayed response was almost choked out. Her tone was heartfelt, but she sounded almost apologetic. "But I wasn't good enough for driving lessons, not good enough for riding school. Not good enough to keep Foxie for. Not good enough to take on vacations. Not quite good enough for anything special. I always blamed it on Dad, but you were part of that, too. It hurts, still."

"Oh honey, I'm sorry."

"Don't *honey* me. Don't talk like Mom." But Amy's tide of anger subsided. She leaned hard into her sister's embrace. Stacey noticed she had grown taller in the last few months. Amy didn't want to be the baby sister any more. Stacey realized she'd have to let go of that. Amy was going to take up the cause, but in her own way this time. Stacey was terrified, and thrilled.

*** ***

"What are you going to do when Golsch asks you to support his no-minimum wage bill?" Grant edged closer to her in the living room, but he was keeping on safe ground by talking politics.

"I don't know. I don't think I can vote to repeal the minimum wage."

"Then Golsch'll probably drop you. And Liotech can't support your campaigns indefinitely, I'm sure."

"Yeah. It's going to be rough."

Another awkward silence. Grant moved away.

Stacey walked over and hugged Kendrick. A short, appropriate hug, but even this embarrassed him. He smiled sideways at her as he slid away.

Then she pulled Corinne aside and put a hand on each shoulder, looking her up and down, then staring in those steady green eyes for a long minute. "You are a model."

"Yeah, right."

"No, you are a model. A real model. I mean it. I swear. You are the person I'm going to talk to my daughter about. You are the kind of woman I want her to try to be."

Corinne just blushed.

*** ***

For the moment, she had no place to live but the condo in Topeka where she and Roland had made love many times. She hated to sleep in the bed she had shared with him, but she didn't have much choice. Amy and Kendrick were staying at Randy's house for the moment, and Audrey and Ruth were staying at the shelter. She wanted to be alone, or at least as alone as she could be in that haunted apartment where so much had gone so wrong. But how alone would she ever be? Driving home, Stacey experienced a waking dream about all the men in her life. She was surrounded by them in the car. The images of their faces faded in and out on all the car's windows, changing positions, changing colors, changing roles. They were all trying to talk to her at the same time, but their voices were garbled. She tried to talk, but they weren't listening. She couldn't hear anything clearly. They didn't hear her. Some men were strong enough to be afraid of but not strong enough to be relied on. Some were strong and silent. Some filled a need within her without needing her at all. Some had raw needs pouring out that she couldn't satisfy. She was confused, frustrated, but she didn't exactly want their faces to go away. She didn't know for sure what she really wanted from them.

She was glad her baby would be a girl.

Coming Soon:

A New God in Town
Book 2 of the Red State/Blue State Confessions

As Stacey gains an unexpected ally in the Kansas legislature and Grant and Lacee test the blue state rules about love, Ruth sets off on a dangerous quest to rescue her sister from captivity.

Thomas Keech has written four previous critically acclaimed novels dealing with state politics, teenagers entangled in suburban corruption, college romance, and a predatory physician. He sincerely hopes this near-dystopian novel of fundamentalist madness is not predictive of the future. He currently lives in a very blue state that has its own problems. He hopes to visit Kansas some day.

CPSIA information can be obtained
at www.ICGtesting.com
Printed in the USA
FSHW021210151019